Alone at l.

"I wanted to have you all to myself," Fin said as he drew Cathy down next to him on the bed. Heat flared through her at the glow in his eyes.

"No one can disturb us now," she whispered, moving closer.

His thumbs slid up her rib cage, grazed the undersides of her breasts, then he lowered his mouth. The friction of the silk camisole and his probing tongue created a delicious ache in her.

Thump . . . thump . . . thump . . .

Was that her heart or Fin's, Cathy wondered dazedly. She moaned as Fin kissed the hollow of her throat.

Thump . . . thump . . . thump . . .

No. It wasn't her heart. Or Fin's. The noise was coming from downstairs.

Thump . . . thump . . . thump . . .

It couldn't be, Cathy wanted to scream. Her suspicions were going up in smoke. Fin was here with her. Who—or what— was downstairs?

When we find a mystery with a Gothic touch that includes screwball comedy, ghostly apparitions and sophisticated writing, then we have another terrific book that breaks the rules—and has to be an Editor's Choice.

Talented and popular Lynn Michaels, who writes romantic suspense, Regencies and mainstream fiction, has penned a delightful tale of a very eccentric family, unlikely noises in the night and a hero who isn't quite what he seems to be. In fact, a lot isn't what it seems to be....

Give in to Temptation, turn the page and enjoy. As always, we would love to receive your comments on this Editor's Choice. Please take time to write us at the address below. Happy reading!

The Editors
Harlequin Temptation
225 Duncan Mill Road
Don Mills, Ontario, Canada
M3B 3K9

Remembrance
LYNN MICHAELS

Harlequin Books

TORONTO • NEW YORK • LONDON
AMSTERDAM • PARIS • SYDNEY • HAMBURG
STOCKHOLM • ATHENS • TOKYO • MILAN

To Judy and Marie

Published June 1990

ISBN 0-373-25404-0

1

THOUGH NINE YEARS HAD PASSED since she'd been to her grandmother's house on Martha's Vineyard, Cathy Martin had no trouble spotting its blue shingled roof, the only portion of the house visible from the coastal highway, or the driveway winding between the sand dunes screening the house from the sea. On the ferry over from Wood's Hole, she'd taken the hardtop off her red MG, and as she eased the Midget through the first curve in the driveway, the offshore wind whipped sand in her eyes as it hissed through the salt grass clinging to the dunes with Yankee tenacity.

Cathy had learned that memory diminishes things, but the house looked just as big and stately as she remembered. The canary-yellow boardwalk ran across the lawn from the front porch to the scratchy gray ribbon of beach. Many things had changed during the years she'd lived in London, but Cathy was glad her grandmother's house wasn't one of them.

She had changed most of all, but Cathy was unaware of all but the most obvious physical alterations. She was twenty-seven now, weighed ten pounds more than she had at eighteen and her once near-platinum hair had darkened to a dull, she believed, ash-blond. She no longer had a figure or a husband, just a tummy trimmer and a divorce decree. And a faint suspicion that her life wasn't quite as together as she thought.

Once she'd parked the MG at the bottom of the sloping driveway, slid out from behind the wheel and pushed the door shut with her hip, Cathy screened her eyes with both hands and surveyed Cat's House—the closest her grandmother had ever come to giving her miniature estate a name. The title offended some of the stuffier islanders but it surprised no one who knew Catherine Lindsay, the long-retired but still-revered Belle of Broadway. Her love for puns and spoonerisms was legendary.

Two stories high with an attic and a widow's walk, the house was built of traditional Cape Cod clapboard in 1853 by Captain Ezekiel Croft, as renowned in his day for his whaling exploits as Cat Lindsay was for her exploits on and off the stage. The quarter-mile grounds included a separate three-car garage, which had once been the stables, a gardener's cottage, a greenhouse, a lath house, a guest house and a gazebo ringed by roses.

As Cathy glanced toward the white-railed fence enclosing the garden, she saw Hadley Archer, her grandmother's antiquarian gardener, look up from the hybrid teas. Wondering if he'd remember her, she waved.

Had stared at her a moment, then leaned the pruners he held against the fence and fished a pipe from the pocket of his tattered gabardine jacket. Next he took a worn leather tobacco pouch from the pocket of his muddy-kneed gray trousers, opened it and began filling his pipe.

This was the signal Cathy remembered from childhood summers spent at Cat's House. She could sit on the fence and watch Had work as long as she watched in silence. When he pulled out his pipe it meant he was finished and it was okay to talk. Smiling, Cathy walked across the lawn, swung herself up on the fence and leaned against one of the posts.

"Hello, Had. Is Grandma in the greenhouse?"

"Nope." He refolded the pouch and tucked it in his back pocket. "Miz Linzay left some while ago."

"Oh." Cathy sighed, disappointed. "Where'd she go?"

"Dunno. Took off with that actor feller."

There was no point asking which "actor feller." Had could recite the Latin and common name of every cultivated and native plant variety on the Vineyard, but the names of the theatrical notables who vacationed on the island and took sporadic turns paying homage to Cat Lindsay were as foreign to him as *Prunus maritima* would be to one of them.

"Oh, well." Cathy sighed again, looked down the rows of rose bushes which were just beginning to bud and asked, "Which one's 'Catherine Lindsay'?"

"Those six there." Had nodded at two tricorner plantings flanking the gate. "Put 'em there so's they'd be the first bloom you see."

"How's it feel to be a famous hybridizer?"

"Lotta to-do if you ask me." Had turned his back to the breeze blowing off the beach, snapped the tip off a wooden match with his thumbnail and lit his pipe. "Don't understand all the hoopla m'self, 'bout the rose or Miz Linzay's memoirs. Fer three, four weeks after word come out she was gonna write a book, the place was crawlin' with folks, mostly show-biz mucky-mucks come out t'see if they was gonna be mentioned or t'make sure they wasn't.

"Then," he continued, pointing a muddy index finger at her, "all of them fellers yer father hired to help Miz Linzay write the book started showin' up. Seemed like ever' week there was a differ'nt one. Spent most m'time pickin' 'em up at the ferry, drivin' 'em back a few days later, pickin' up another one, drivin' 'im back. High-strung bunch. Worse'n Miz Linzay's actin' friends. Even that Mr. Penney. Always seemed real steady, but 'e was goosier than the whole lot of 'em." Had shook his head, his dentures clicking on the stem of his pipe. "You s'pose you can get Miz Linzay's book written, Cathy?"

"That's why I'm here," she answered confidently.

"You only wrote one book," Had replied pointedly. "Some kinda novel, wasn't it?"

That was more or less what the critics had said, too, and though her shoulders sagged, Cathy gave Had a plucky smile. "I'm sure I can do it. And so is my father."

Had snorted ruefully. "Yer father thought all them other fellers could, too. T'the man, they all lit outta here glassy eyed an' mumblin' t'themselves."

"All them other fellers" totaled eight and each was a highly regarded author. Especially Noel Penney, her father's oldest, dearest friend, who'd two years ago won a Pulitzer prize for *Phineas's Rainbow*, the biography of Phineas Martin, Cat's long-dead husband and the grandfather Cathy had never known.

When her mother had written her that Noel was going to coauthor her grandmother's memoirs, Cathy had thought them the perfect team. Her father hadn't mentioned the other seven fellers when he'd called her in London and cajoled her into taking a crack at the book; he'd saved them until she'd come home to Boston three days ago. And now that she recalled the conversation, Cathy realized her father had been uncharacteristically vague; that he had, in fact, looked a bit glassy eyed. He'd even mumbled once or twice.

Uh-oh, she thought.

"Now that you mention it, Had, my father wasn't terribly clear about the turnover in coauthors. What exactly was the problem?"

"Wouldn't know." Had knocked the ash out of his pipe and put it back in his pocket. "Don't mix in Miz Linzay's personal business. Jus' tend the garden."

Hadley Archer had been just tending the garden and mixing into as much of Cat's personal business as he could since Cathy was ten years old. What he'd just told her convinced her her father had been deliberately evasive. She smiled at his disclaimer and slid off the fence.

"See you later, Had," she said and turned toward the driveway.

"I think Miz Linzay wanted you to write her memoirs all along."

Cathy had taken only a few steps when Had offered this opinion, and she turned back to look at him. "Why me?"

"She knows you ain't afraid of ghosts."

A slow shiver started up Cathy's spine, then one corner of Had's mouth twitched, and she laughed. "Oh, I get it. I'm not afraid of ghosts—or ghostwriting. Pretty good, Had. See you later."

Pursing her lips thoughtfully, Cathy walked back to her car. Eccentric though Had was, he was also as stalwart and honest as her father was sophisticated and facile. Lindsay Martin was not only a playwright but a playwright's son, so his words were obviously well chosen.

Her father was also manipulative, but she wouldn't let this trouble her. At least not until she'd unloaded the car, had a drink and a chance to call him.

Stumbling under the weight of two suitcases that had seemed a lot lighter when she'd strapped them onto the luggage rack in Boston, Cathy was halfway up the flagstone patio steps when the Dutch back door swung open. Helmut, three hundred pounds if he was an ounce, his heavily tattooed arms crossed on the lower half of the door, leaned outside to watch her. Not to offer to help, just to watch.

"Hi, ya, Cath. Yer early."

"I got—" She gasped, pausing on the second step from the top to catch her breath "—an early start."

"Those look heavy. Better get 'em in here 'fore you drop 'em." Helmut unlatched the door, swung it open and disappeared inside.

"Some people never change," Cathy panted as she struggled with the cases across the patio, wrestled them through the door and dropped them with a thud in the middle of the kitchen floor.

"Hear you lost weight," Helmut said as he turned away from the sink and handed her a glass of water. "'Bout a hunnard and eighty pounds of ham."

Helmut meant her ex-husband Garrett Pauling—the next Olivier, as he liked to call himself—and though Cathy was sick to death of divorce jokes, she smiled good-naturedly as Helmut's booming laugh rattled the copper saucepans hung on the white tile wall behind the stove. Then she drank the water and gave the glass back to him.

"Had said Grandma took off with some actor. Anybody I know?"

"Nah. Jus' that bum what lives down the beach."

"D'you know when she'll be home?"

"Whenever she wears 'im out. You got any more luggage?"

"Yes." Cathy's voice and her expression brightened hopefully. "Two more, plus my computer."

"Better leave 'em till later, then. Those stairs are a killer."

"Why, thank you, Helmut," she replied with an overlarge smile. "How thoughtful."

As she picked up her suitcases and headed for the main staircase in the dining room, Cathy wondered how Helmut—who as far as she knew hadn't been up it in the nearly two dozen years he'd worked for Cat Lindsay—had discovered the stairs were a killer.

On the landing twenty steps up from the first floor, Cathy took another rest stop. Here the staircase split into two flights of twenty more steps each and formed the square second-floor gallery overhanging the living room and dining room. Sunshine poured through the round leaded glass window high above her as she breathed deeply and looked up at the gleaming oak banisters enclosing the gallery. They'd been constructed, scaled down to fit the house, from the railings on the *Rachel Simms*, Captain Croft's whaling ship.

Rachel Simms, the daughter of a New Bedford merchant, had been his fiancée. Though he'd named his ship for her, old Zeke hadn't been very eager to settle down, and Rachel got fed up after ten years of waiting and married somebody else while Zeke and his crew were at sea. When he returned to port and found Rachel married, Captain Croft had been so heartbroken he'd scavenged and then scuttled the *Rachel Simms* somewhere off the Vineyard. Nobody knew where, not even the captain's maiden great-niece, from whom Cat Lindsay had bought the house.

Growing up, Cathy had thought the story so romantic. She'd daydreamed about finding a piece of the *Rachel Simms* washed up on the beach, and had spent rainy days in the attic poring through the captain's papers, all carefully stowed away in musty old sea trunks left behind by his niece.

She hadn't cared about the maps and charts she'd found; she'd been looking for love letters from Rachel. She'd never found any, and now, as she drew a deep breath and launched herself, arms shuddering, up the right-hand staircase, Cathy cursed Captain Croft for building such a damn big ship, and then such a damn big house to accommodate its bits and pieces.

The bedroom she always slept in, which shared the widow's walk, a bathroom and a sitting room with her grandmother's bedroom, was at the far end of the gallery. Other than the tangy pine smell of a cleaner and fresh sheets on the turned-down double four-poster, the room hadn't been altered since her last summer in residence at Cat's House, the summer she'd turned eighteen, the summer she'd met Garrett.

Playbills from her father's shows all but obscured the full-length mirror on the closet door, posters of the Doobie Brothers, Kansas and Foreigner clung to the blue walls on thin strips of yellowed adhesive tape and a stuffed Snoopy lay on the bed. Cathy hadn't remembered leaving so much junk behind, hadn't any idea that her grandmother would enshrine it, or that it would suddenly make her feel so old and disjointed. But that's how she felt, old, disjointed and out of place.

According to her assertiveness training, large-muscle exercise was the best way to combat feelings of inadequacy. Twenty minutes later, after she'd hauled her other suitcases and her crated PC upstairs and flung herself, heart thumping, on the bed, Cathy thought a better way to deal with insecurity would be a tall, dark and handsome paramedic well trained in the more titillating aspects of CPR. Since one wasn't handy, she sat up and wondered what she was going to do with herself until her grandmother came home.

She could clear all this junk out of her room and lug it up to the attic, but she'd had enough exercise for one day.

She thought another moment or so, then decided to take to the beach with *Phineas's Rainbow*. Noel Penney was apt to show up, and since she'd told him in the thank-you she'd written him two years ago when he'd sent her an autographed copy that she'd absolutely loved the book, she supposed she ought to read it.

Tugging the wedding-ring quilt off the bed and putting on her sunglasses, Cathy made for the beach with her grandfather's biography tucked in the crook of her arm. Once she'd cleared of the dunes that protected Cat's House, the raw April wind streamed her hair behind her and raised gooseflesh on her arms inside the sleeves of her lightweight sweater. Flinging the quilt around her, she huddled into it and trudged along looking for a sheltered spot to read in.

A half mile or so down the beach she found a small windblown dune that would probably be gone after the next big storm and hunkered down behind it. Though the midday sun had disappeared behind a thin scud of gray cloud, the sand was still warm, and Cathy sighed as she wiggled her back into it. Her goose bumps receded, the wind buffeted in her ears and sand skittered around her as she leaned *Phineas's Rainbow* against her drawn-up knees and looked at her grandfather's picture on the back cover.

It was a black-and-white glossy taken when he was thirty-five, some twenty-two years before Cathy was born. He'd been outrageously handsome, a dark-haired, blue-eyed three-way tie between Cary Grant, Errol Flynn and John Barrymore, who'd starred on Broadway in two of his plays.

Catherine Lindsay had been the love of his life. He'd met Cat in his mother-in-law's parlor in Boston on a sunny October afternoon in 1927, six months after he'd married her first cousin, Alma. He'd slept with her that night, dumped Alma in the morning and, after lunch, had caught the New York via Philadelphia train with Cat. Cathy had never been able to figure out exactly who had corrupted whom, but knowing her grandmother, she'd always felt pretty sure that Phineas had been the corruptee.

"You poor jerk." Cathy smiled and traced her grandfather's dimpled chin with her index finger. "You never had a chance."

And neither had she once she'd married Garrett. It had taken Cathy nine years to realize he'd not only swept her off her feet, but swept away her identity as well—what little she'd managed to accumulate growing up in a family of congenital overachievers, rolling around for eighteen years in their genetically gifted midst like a lost ball in high weeds. Garrett hadn't understood that, couldn't comprehend why streaming along in the wake of his helicon talent wasn't enough for her.

Cathy hadn't been able to explain it to him, either, so she'd left. First Garrett, and then London, afraid that she'd cave in and go back to him, afraid that she'd never amount to anything on her own, afraid that she'd settle for being a poorly packed snowball tumbling along in the tail of somebody else's avalanche.

Scary as it was, she'd made the right decision. But what about her grandfather? Had he ever had regrets? Had he ever wished he'd stayed with Alma? According to her grandmother, who'd been known to lie pathologically when it suited her best interests, he never had. Yet Cathy wondered.

The sun came out from behind the clouds and the wind died as she opened the book to page 146, just before grandfather's cataclysmic meeting with her grandmother. Lulled by the warm sand and the sun on her face, she began to nod off in the middle of the third paragraph on page

149. Riveting prose, Noel, she thought sleepily as she let *Phineas's Rainbow* fall open against her chest and her eyes drift shut.

When Cathy jerked awake, she was curled on her left side with the quilt tangled around her, her sunglasses askew and the book half under her head with one corner of it digging into her cheek. Groaning she rolled stiffly onto her back, started to yawn and stretch, then froze as she looked up and saw her grandfather standing in front of her.

Leaning toward her, he wrapped his hands around his thighs just above his knees and smiled. He had on stone-washed jeans and a black, V neck cable-knit sweater that was almost the same color as the dark hair falling over his navy-blue eyes. With his right hand he reached out and lightly grazed his knuckles across the crease in her cheek.

"Next time you want to nap on the beach, pussy willow," he said, "call me and I'll loan you my shoulder."

The brush of his knuckles was so light, so barely there, that Cathy felt nothing. Of course not, she thought dazedly, because he isn't here, he isn't real, no matter how alive he looks.

"Y-you're dead," she stammered.

His smile widened as he leaned closer, near enough for Cathy to see the dark hair on his chest as the wind gusted and ruffled his hair around his ears. "Do I look dead?"

His baritone voice had a soft, lilting cadence to it that Cathy had heard before but couldn't identify.

"I'm going to close my eyes," she said, "and very slowly count to ten. When I open them, you're going to be gone."

"Whatever you say, pussy willow."

His voice made her shiver as she closed her eyes, covered them with her hands, and started counting.

"Eight—nine—ten," she finished, spreading her fingers and opening her eyes.

He was gone.

Thrashing her way out of the tangled quilt, Cathy leaped to her feet. The wind lashed her hair into her eyes as she looked up and down the almost quarter mile of empty beach in both directions and felt herself start to tremble.

Where the hell had he gone? Or better yet, she wondered where he had come from—her imagination, or had she been dreaming? If so, he was the most vivid dream she'd ever had.

Never again, so help her God, would she dream, Cathy vowed, snatching up the quilt, her sunglasses, *Phineas's Rainbow*, and running for Cat's House. She didn't stop until she was in her bedroom, the door shut behind her, her shoulder blades pressed against it and her heart thudding in her chest. So much for Hadley Archer and his theory that she wasn't afraid of ghosts.

But she hadn't seen a ghost. Ghosts wore old sheets and moaned. And so did Cathy, pressing one hand to her throat at the remembrance of long, well-muscled legs in jeans so tight they looked as if they'd been spray painted on. She'd had a dream. Too much caffeine or not enough sleep was creating hallucinations.

There was, after all, no such thing as ghosts.

Cathy kept telling herself that as she sat on the edge of the bed staring at *Phineas's Rainbow*, lying front cover up on the floor where she'd dropped it, the dust jacket askew and wrinkled. It's only a book, she told herself, pick it up and straighten it. She did, slowly and gingerly, unaware that she was holding her breath until Helmut's booming voice thundered, "Lunch!" and she let the book fly with a startled yelp. It slammed into the pine headboard with a thwack, plopped onto the pillow, slid lopsidedly off the percale case and thudded to the floor between the bed and the wall.

It could stay there until hell froze over, she decided. Her heart trip hammering between her ribs again, Cathy took a deep breath and went downstairs.

2

WHEN CATHY ENTERED the dining room, her grandmother, dressed in a pink jogging suit, was seated at the table eating clam chowder.

"My darling girl!" Cat cried, throwing her stick-thin arms wide as Cathy bent over her chair and kissed her mouth.

Her grandmother smelled of tobacco, peppermint—to mask the tobacco—perfume and hair spray. Her shock of wispy white hair looked whiter and her sapphire-blue eyes more watery than Cathy remembered. The tip of her long nose sagged a bit, but for eighty-seven, she thought Cat looked terrific.

"Where were you this morning, Grandma?" Cathy asked as she slid into her chair.

"Where else would I be with a handsome young man fifty years my junior?" Cat wagged her eyebrows wickedly. "I was walking all over Edgartown making people wonder if he sleeps with me."

"Does he?"

"Hell, no! What does he want with an old bone heap? But the villagers don't know that."

"Grandma." Cathy tsked and picked up her spoon. "Did you have a good time?"

"Darling girl." Cat gave her a Cheshire cat smile. "I *always* have a good time."

When they'd finished their chowder, Cathy carried their coffee into the living room. She and Cat sat cross-legged on the window seat, facing each other and sharing an ashtray. Cathy loved to smoke, but only allowed herself two cigarettes a day—one after lunch and one after supper.

"So tell me, darling girl," Cat said. "What did you do this morning?"

Cathy's attention caught the pencil-thin line of smoke curling from the tip of her cigarette in a vaguely human shape. It reminded her of the dream she'd had and made her shiver. Her grandmother, who'd spent nine months of her early career in vaudeville as Harry Houdini's assistant and had picked up some of her more bizarre views on metaphysics from the great escape artist, was probably a poor person to regale with her experience, but she had to tell someone.

"I went out to the beach to read and fell asleep," Cathy told her. "I had a dream, the most vivid one I've ever had. I was reading *Phineas's Rainbow*, you see, and when I woke up—I mean, when I woke up in the dream—Granddad was standing there smiling at me."

Hands cupped around her knees, her cigarette in the fluted shell ashtray drifting smoke toward the window, Cat sat looking at Cathy as if she'd just grown another head.

"It sounds silly now telling you," she went on hurriedly, wishing she'd never started and putting out her cigarette, "but he looked so alive it scared me half to death. I closed my eyes, counted to ten and when I opened them he was gone. Naturally, because he wasn't really there. I mean he couldn't have been, because he's dead."

Isn't he? Cathy felt compelled to ask, but didn't.

"Of course he's dead." Cat took a drag of her cigarette, blew smoke over her shoulder and smiled indulgently. "You have such an incredible imagination, darling girl."

Silently Cathy agreed, feeling like an absolute idiot, and sheepishly returned her grandmother's smile. "Comes in handy when I write, though."

"Ah, yes—writing!" With a Bette Davis flourish of her filtered cigarette, Cat leaned forward eagerly. "I'm so excited about my memoirs, darling girl, and so delighted you're going to be my ghostwriter—"

"Excuse me, Grandma, coauthor."

"Same thing," she replied, dribbling ash across the rose chintz window seat as she gave a dismissive wave.

"Not quite," Cathy corrected her. "A ghostwriter takes no credit. A coauthor shares the bill."

Cat arched one eyebrow. "Oh?"

"Second billing, of course," Cathy assured her. "Beneath the title the jacket will read—in very *large* type— 'by Catherine Lindsay.' Underneath your name—in very *small* type—it will say 'with Catherine Lindsay Martin.'"

"Ah, well, then." Cat beamed. "We've got the whole of the afternoon. What say we begin?"

"Great. Just let me get my things."

It took Cathy five minutes to collect her cassette recorder, a spiral notebook and two disposable automatic pencils. She returned to the living room where Cat had pulled aside the sheer window panel with her left hand and sat gazing somewhat vacantly at the beach, her thin gold wedding band shining dully in the feeble sun. Over her grandmother's shoulder, Cathy saw that the sky had darkened and the sea had begun to swell ominously toward shore.

"We'll have rain before supper." Cat let the panel fall, drew her knees into the circle of her arms and vigorously chafed her shins. "These old joints never fail me, you know. Since I took that tumble backstage at the Shubert, my weather predictions have been as accurate as any druid's. Years later I had a gallbladder attack and the doctor told me I'd dislocated the right knee at some point in my life. Well, you know, darling girl, it hurt like the dickens when I fell. I was on my way to the wings from my dressing room—in those days theaters were so dark—for act 2, scene 3 of *She Stoops to Conquer*, and brother, did I stoop!"

Slapping the heels of her hands on her knees, Cat threw back her head and let go a peal of her wonderfully raunchy laughter. On both her wrists plastic bangles and gold manacle bracelets clicked together; around her neck heaps of gold chains, heavy with trinkets and amulets, bounced against her chest.

"Do you know what I fell over? A corset stay! Three inches of whalebone! Harmless enough in a corset, but bloody murder on the floor in pitch darkness! Well, down I went and up I came in *agony*! But what could I do? It was my *cue*! I gave the knee a good punch and went on!"

Cat grinned in triumph. Cathy smiled, she hoped not condescendingly.

"That's a great story, Grandma, but it's been quoted in at least a dozen other places. I think we should start someplace else."

"Oh, do you? Very well, then. Let me think a moment."

While Cat, her lips pursed thoughtfully, tapped her left index finger on her chin, Cathy settled herself in the rose velvet wing chair next to the window seat, opened her notebook and switched on the recorder.

"How's this?" Cat asked. "As Phineas told me in bed later that evening—and as I realized the moment our eyes met for the first time across Aunt Elvira's parlor—there was going to be hell to pay."

"Fabulous! Open with the juicy stuff!"

"Juicy stuff?"

"Sex, grandma," Cathy replied, head bent as she made a note to fill in the description of Aunt Elvira's parlor. "It sells books."

"In that case, we should go back a bit farther."

"No, no, let's start with Granddad."

Cathy glanced up in time to see Cat peer somewhat myopically at the face of a pendant watch dangling from one of her chains. She let it fall as Cathy met her gaze, then swung her feet to the floor and lit a cigarette from her pack on the low table in front of the window seat.

"You should go back to the theater, darling girl," she said, abruptly changing subjects. "You really showed great promise."

"I'm much happier writing, Grandma. I'm a nervous wreck in a play. I throw up before I go on."

"Darling, that's *natural*! You wouldn't be great if you weren't high-strung!"

"But, Grandma," Cathy told her with a bemused smile. "I throw up between scenes."

Cat laughed again. "You're so clever and witty! And your *name*, darling girl! It absolutely *screams* to be on a marquee!"

"I stink, Grandma," Cathy told her flatly. "Trying to follow in your footsteps was the first worst mistake I ever made in my life. I hated it. And by the way, did you hate Alma?"

"Heavens, no! But she hated me, I can tell you!" Cat put out her cigarette, placed her hands on her knees and looked squarely at Cathy. "Darling girl, will you promise me something? If I speak to Phineas and he's willing to whip up something for you, will you take it? Not to Broadway if you don't want to, but at least through tryouts?"

Cathy's mouth dropped open and she stared, glassy eyed, at her grandmother.

"You needn't answer now. I can see you're overwhelmed." Cat scrambled back onto the window seat and drew the curtain aside; the sun had brightened, dissipating the heavier clouds, and the sea had quieted. "My God, could my knee be wrong? Oh, well. One failure in sixty years isn't bad. And enough of *this*." She let go of the curtain and glared at the recorder, which was still running. "Besides, I've just remembered an important errand."

That jerked Cathy out of her slack-jawed daze. "But Grandma, we've just started!"

"Oh, we've scads of time, and this mission is top priority! Do you remember that old shack just down the beach, darling girl? You know, the one built up on stilts?"

"Yes, Grandma, I remember it, but—"

"And that stand of pine trees next to it? Yes, of course you do, your memory is marvelous! There's the most *exquisite* piece of driftwood there! You'll know it instantly, darling girl, it's shaped like a snarling saber-toothed tiger poised to spring, and I *must* have it!"

"But Grandma—"

"But nothing!" Cat interrupted huffily. "It's going to rain today, I tell you! Perhaps not by supper, but it *is* going to rain! This storm will be a doozy when it hits. We daren't leave the tiger on the beach and risk it being washed away to Nantucket for some varicose-veined tourist to find." Cat got to her feet and braced both hands on the arms of Cathy's chair. "Trot along now and fetch the tiger home for Grandmama."

Then she squeezed Cathy's cheeks, gave her a smacking kiss on the mouth and swept away, tinkling and clicking.

"Trot!" Cathy exclaimed as she, too, left the room. "That shack must be three miles down the beach!"

"He-e-ell-mm-uu-tt!" Cat shouted from the gap in the waist-high section of quarterdeck rail from the *Rachel Simms*, dividing the living room and dining room, then turned to give Cathy her most dazzling smile. "Darling girl, I'm not sending you on a fool's errand. This is *important*! Phineas has admired the tiger for weeks, wouldn't allow me to touch it, told me to let nature ripen it where it lay. Well, the man is so lazy—much as I *adore* him, he's a layabout. He won't notice this storm coming so I—or rather you—must bring the tiger home before the sea claims him."

Wondering if spirits wrote plays and collected driftwood, Cathy gaped first at her grandmother, then at Helmut looming in the kitchen doorway.

"Did you prepare the hamper?" Cat asked.

"Yeah, here it is." Helmut raised a large wicker picnic basket in his beefy right hand.

Cat strode across the oriental carpet, swept the hamper from him and carried it back to Cathy. Shoving it into her hands, she leaned across the braided handles and looked her squarely in the eye.

"No wonder your marriage was a flop if you don't know that you *never* show up empty-handed for an assignation on the beach." Hooking one hand around Cathy's arm, Cat turned her around and propelled her across the living room. "Men are absolutely *ravenous* after making love on the beach, darling girl, and Phineas more so than most. I promised him you'd be on time, so hurry now or you'll be late." She kicked open the screen door and pushed Cathy out onto the front porch. "Oh, yes, and afterward, don't forget to ask him about the play I want him to write for you."

"Grandma, get a grip—" Cathy sputtered and spun around, but the screen and then the heavy inside door slammed shut in her face.

On reality, she'd meant to say, but couldn't finish the sentence for the lump she suddenly felt in her throat. For a moment she stood there, uncertain what to do. Think, she told her brain, but it refused. Oh, well, she was out here, she might as well—

Oh, God! She was out here—alone! Wide-eyed, Cathy stared at the thin ribbon of beach lying so menacingly empty beyond the boardwalk.

Her assertiveness training manual said the best way to deal with fear was to face it. Brave words, thought Cathy, who couldn't remember so much as a footnote concerning ghosts or anything supernatural.

"I can do this," she said, quaking inside but stepping determinedly onto the sand. "I'll just nip down the beach, grab the tiger and beat it home before anyone even knows I'm out here. Besides, there's no such thing as ghosts."

These brave words gave Cathy courage as she double-timed it past the dunes. Once Cat's House disappeared behind them, and the muscles in her arms began to tremble from the weight of Helmut's hamper, she found a clump of rocks and stowed the waterproof basket behind it.

She wasn't going to dine on the sand with a ghost, and she most certainly wasn't going to make love to one. Phineas was her grandfather, and that was incest. Physical or spiritual, it was still incest.

Despite the spring chill the afternoon was muggy and oppressive. The sun, a small round silver ball, dipped in and out of the gloom. Cathy began to perspire, and her courage began to fail as she thought about her grandmother. Ghosts moaned and rattled chains at midnight in the attic. They didn't write plays or collect driftwood, but eighty-seven-year-old women did become senile.

Had her father cajoled her into coming because he suspected something was wrong? Recalling the conversation she'd had with him in Boston, and his cautions not to overtax but to coddle Cat, it seemed likely, likely enough that Cathy felt tears in her eyes as she considered it. Her pace began to flag along with her spirits, just as the clouds began to sag again and the wind picked up. Sand whipped in her face, but she bent her head against it and slogged purposefully on.

The copse of scrawny pines where Cat said she'd find the driftwood tiger grew a hundred or so yards up the beach from the water. Cathy was sure she remembered the place, and knew she was getting close when she slid down a low dune and stumbled past the weather-beaten old shack Cat had mentioned. Built on foot-high stilts with a terminal case of dry rot, it looked as if it had been here in 1838 when Bartholomew Gosnold had discovered the island. It also looked as though the only thing holding it up was air.

By this time, Cathy was hot, tired and dripping perspiration. She had sand in her sneakers, grit up her nose and she couldn't find a single piece of driftwood that resembled a snarling saber-toothed tiger poised to spring. The wind had turned cold and salty out of the northeast and hissed through the undernourished trees as she wove her way through them.

For a good ten minutes Cathy searched, then gave up. Someone else had already claimed the tiger. And if that someone was Phineas, then he was welcome to it. With her mind on the storm, doubting she'd make it to Cat's House before it hit, Cathy broke out of the pines onto the beach.

The clouds were dark and heavy now, nearly merging with the whitecaps whooshing toward shore with frightening ferocity.

"You're late!"

A voice, all but swallowed by the thundering surf, shouted at Cathy from the direction of the old shack. She froze and felt a slow, icy shiver trickle down her spine.

"I'd gone in, but decided to take another look!" The voice, which sounded eerily familiar, shouted again. "Let's get inside before this storm breaks!"

Holding her breath, Cathy turned around and saw her grandfather striding toward her in cutoffs and a white T-shirt.

"Where's our supper?" he asked, raising his voice above the booming waves. "Helmut was supposed to pack a hamper."

It can't be him, Cathy thought numbly, it just can't.

"Cath?" He stopped a scant yard away from her and cocked his head to one side. "Are you all right?"

No, I'm not, she wanted to say but couldn't. All she could do was stare.

He looked so real. Sand clung to the hair on his bare legs and his naked toes were caked with mud. She'd always thought you could see through ghosts, but this one was solid.

"Hello, Cath," he said, offering his right hand. "I'm Phineas."

I know who you are, she wanted to say, but her voice still wouldn't work. Thunder rumbled and the rush of the wind tore at her hair and his. She heard the musical lilt in his voice and shivered. Her ears started to ring and her knees to tremble.

"What's the matter?" he asked, his eyebrows drawing together. "You look like you've just seen a ghost."

"Oh, no." Cathy moaned weakly. "You had to say it." And then she fainted.

3

A DROP OF COLD WATER splattering across the bridge of her nose jolted Cathy back to consciousness. Her eyes sprang open, but for a moment all she could see through her wet lashes were blurred, smeary shapes. It took several reflexive blinks for her vision to clear; when it did she looked up at her grandfather's face.

He was smiling at her, his dark hair wet and dripping, the front of his white T-shirt spattered with raindrops.

"Am I dead?" she asked in a small voice.

"No," he said gently. "You fainted."

Blinking again, Cathy turned her head and looked around her. She was lying on the floor, on a faded patchwork quilt near a crumbling stone fireplace.

"Where am I?"

"In my cabin."

"Where's that? On the Other Side?"

"No," he said, chuckling. "On the beach."

Her brain felt fuzzy, but cleared suddenly as her senses returned and she realized that the warm and firm cushion the back of her head rested on was his thigh. She felt faint again, swallowed hard and swept one arm over her eyes.

"I think you could use a good, strong cup of tea," he said, and eased her out of his lap.

A good stiff drink sounded better, but Cathy didn't say so. Instead, as she sank onto something soft that smelled vaguely of bleach, she raised her arm and saw that he'd shifted her onto two bed pillows. She took another look

around, saw that the entire cabin wasn't much bigger than
the bathroom she shared with her grandmother, then
turned her head and watched the man who said his name
was Phineas tear two tea bags out of their envelopes and
drop them into stoneware mugs.

While he poured boiling water from a battered kettle on
a camp stove set on top of a small counter beside the back
door, Cathy examined the open cupboards above his
head. Between an assortment of dented aluminum pans
stood boxes of cookies and cereal; cans of soup, tomato
and chicken noodle; and a half-empty five-pound bag of
sugar.

Although she wasn't sure whether or not ectoplasm was
solid, she was ninety-nine percent sure ghosts did not re-
quire food to sustain life. Therefore the tall, dark-haired
man making her a cup of tea was real, not a dream or a
delusion, and definitely not her grandfather. Who he was
and why he looked like Phineas Martin's clone she didn't
yet know, but the rush of relief she felt was almost as tan-
gible as the storm crashing and booming outside.

Sitting up slowly, Cathy looked over her shoulder at the
deep, heavy gloom pressing against the small window in
the wall near the front door. Needles of rain pelted the
glass, the wind howled and thunder rumbled ever closer
as the nor'easter rolled ashore.

"Is this the old shed on the beach?" she asked, glancing
over the meager furnishings: a tweed couch full of holes
and a mismatched table and chair with an old manual
typewriter on top of it. "The one that looks like the only
thing holding it up is air?"

"That's about all that is." He gave Cathy a bemused
smile as she turned toward him and he bent over an ice
chest on the floor. "Milk or sugar?"

"Both, please."

"Let's take it from the top, shall we?" He stirred sugar into the mugs with a soupspoon, picked them up and carried them to the quilt. "I'm Phineas McGraw, Fin for short."

Cathy could've kissed him. Not for the cup of tea he handed her as he sat down beside her, but for having the same name as her grandfather. Her mind was intact. Giddy with relief, Cathy laughed until tears ran down her cheeks and the mug in her hands shook and sloshed hot tea on her fingers.

"I'm glad you think it's funny," Fin McGraw said good-naturedly as he watched her put the cup down and wipe her hands on her jeans. "I've always thought it an awful old name myself."

"Oh, it is—I mean, it isn't—I mean—"

Catching herself in midsentence, Cathy looked at the very real, very handsome man smiling at her. Did she really want to tell him she'd thought he was a ghost? Maybe on their twenty-fifth wedding anniversary.

"It isn't funny," she said, "it's just that my grandfather's name was Phineas."

"I know." He took a healthy swig from his mug, then put it down on the quilt next to hers. "Cat mentions it frequently."

"Maybe because you're a playwright, too."

Thunder rolled, rattling the window and trembling the floor. Fin raised one eyebrow, stood on his knees to reach the wood box next to the fireplace and tossed several pieces of driftwood onto the cold ashes.

"I'm an actor. I play the Rosebriar on Nantucket every summer. That's why I'm here. Rehearsals start in three weeks."

"Oh, really? I could've sworn Grandma said you were a playwright."

"You must've misunderstood," he said, crumpling pages of the *Vineyard Gazette* and stuffing them under the logs.

Cathy knew she hadn't but chose not to argue the point. At least not with Fin McGraw.

"Guess I must have," she replied.

Smiling at her over his shoulder, Fin struck a match from a box on the floor. The sea-bleached wood caught almost as quickly as the newsprint, sparking and popping, filling the cabin with salt-tinged smoke.

"Would you by any chance happen to be the 'actor feller' Grandma was out with this morning?"

"I am." He grinned as he fed smaller pieces of wood into the hissing blue flames. "Rather nice of old Helmut. Usually he calls me that bum what lives down the beach."

Cathy noticed how he said "whot" instead of "what." "That is what Helmut called you," she replied. "Had referred to you as that 'actor feller.'"

"Good old Helmut." He chuckled. "Does he like anybody?"

"My grandmother. Beyond that, I don't think so."

"By the way, I rescued Cat's tiger." Fin reached into the wood box, pulled out the gnarled driftwood and handed it to Cathy as he sat back on the quilt beside her. "When you hadn't shown up by two o'clock, I figured Cat had lost her touch and you weren't coming."

"Touch?" Cathy echoed.

"If she hadn't gone on the stage, she'd've made one helluva used-car salesman, your grandmother." He picked up his mug and drained it, then set it aside and leaned toward her on his left arm. "What convinced you to come? My blue eyes or my sexy-as-hell Irish accent?"

His voice dropped about half an octave as he edged closer to her and brushed his shoulder against hers. Cathy wondered what the chances were this wasn't a pass. Slim and none, she decided, but just in case, she pinned a friendly smile on her face as she picked up the tiger and used it as a fulcrum to pry him away from her.

"My grandmother convinced me to come—for *this*."

Glancing down at the chunk of driftwood wedged between them, then at Cathy's face, Fin took the hint and withdrew.

"I'm trying to make up for scaring you this morning."

"You didn't scare me," she denied, a little too sharply.

"The hell I didn't. You said, 'You're dead—'" He stopped suddenly, studied her face intently, then went on puzzledly. "And when you came around just now you asked me if *you* were—"

A slow, incredulous smile spread across his face. Hoping she could stonewall and bluff, Cathy raised her chin disdainfully and said nothing.

"No wonder you fainted when I said you looked like you'd seen a ghost." He chuckled, then his smile gave way to a grin. "You thought you had."

"How utterly ridiculous—" Cathy began huffily.

But it was too late. She'd heard the expression "roll on the floor with laughter," but she'd never seen anybody do it until Fin keeled over on his back and howled, his melodious baritone spiraling into a high *C* laugh.

Crimson with humiliation, Cathy listened to him laugh louder than the shriek of the storm gaining force outside. Justifiable homicide, she decided. That's what it would be if she clubbed him to death with the driftwood tiger.

"Jesus, Mary and all the saints in heaven." He sighed at length, still chuckling, but able at least to sit up and draw a deep breath. "You're lucky I'm mad about you and have a sense of humor, Cath. Otherwise I'd be showing you the door about now, storm or no storm."

As if on cue, wicked green lightning flashed, thunder boomed and the shed quivered on its flimsy foundations. Water began to leak from the ceiling near the fireplace, and Cathy could've sworn she smelled sulfur.

"Mad about me? You don't even know me! And what was I supposed to think when you vanished into thin air?"

"Who vanished?" Fin retorted. "I ducked behind the other side of the dune. What I'd like to know is just who the bloody hell did you think I was? Or should I say *wasn't*?"

"Oh, how droll," Cathy shot back nastily. "I just adore Irish whimsy."

His jaw tightened and he frowned. "Now see here, Cath—"

"Cathy. My name is *Cathy*."

"Cat, Cath, Cathy, what's in a name? That which we call a rose by any other—"

A second eerie flash of lightning interrupted his recitation from act 2, scene 2 of *Romeo and Juliet*. Instant ear-splitting thunder shuddered through the walls and the floor. The boards groaned, and Cathy heard it, then—the insidious hiss of water moving under the cabin.

"What in bloody hell," Fin muttered, getting to his feet and crossing to the front window.

With the tiger still in her hand, Cathy followed. Crowded next to him, she saw evergreen boughs floating on the gray storm-tossed ocean just outside the door. Lightning forked above the foam-headed breakers swelling where the copse of scrawny pines had grown. White-caps peeled back to hurl themselves at the beach, and gooseflesh sprang everywhere on Cathy's body as she realized the beach now lay beyond the shed. Her feet were wet, and she glanced down at the foam seeping beneath the door and spouting through the cracks in the floor-boards.

"Egad, Mr. Christian, we're taking on water." Fin stamped his bare toes in the puddle pooling around their feet. "Man the life boats, we're abandoning ship."

"Abandoning ship for where, Captain Bligh?" Cathy asked, following him as he crossed the cabin to the back door.

"My Jeep. It's parked just up the beach."

The wind caught the door as he opened it, and slammed it against the outside wall of the cabin. The rain drove so hard Cathy could just barely see the frothing gray water churning beyond the threshold.

"How far is it?"

"About a hundred yards." He frowned as another wave struck and the cabin shuddered again. "I knew I should have replaced those bloody rotten stilts."

"You don't think they'll hold?"

In answer, a fresh leak sprang like a geyser at Cathy's feet, thoroughly soaking her up to her knees.

"What d'you think?" Fin returned.

"I think," Cathy replied, "that if we stay here, we'll end washed up on Nantucket in time for tea."

"My thoughts exactly," he agreed and took the tiger away from her.

Drawing back his arm, he gave it a mighty heave, then clamped his right hand like a vice around her left wrist and jumped. They landed, splashing and stumbling, in frigid knee-deep water. The jolt took Cathy's breath away, and Fin almost pulled her arm out of its socket as he lunged, towing her behind him, up the beach.

Though they tried, the deep water and the loose, suck-ing sand beneath it made running impossible. The only advantage they had was the fifty-mile-an-hour wind howling at their backs, but even that failed as the next breaker crashed ashore, roared up the beach and snatched Cathy out of Fin's grasp.

The wave picked her up, hurled her forward and slammed her down face first. Then it slid away with an almost human sigh, leaving her draped with seaweed and choking on saltwater. Wobbling up on her knees, Cathy peeled kelp out of her face and saw Fin, a dozen yards behind her, trying to claw his way out of the undertow curled around his knees and dragging him back down the beach.

Sliding her way to him, Cathy threw herself the last couple of feet and landed on her stomach with her hands locked around his wrists. For no more than two seconds her weight was enough to counterbalance the pull of the wave, long enough for Fin to raise his sand-caked face and shout, "Run!"

Cathy ignored him, struggled to sit up and hang on as the undertow started to suck her, too, toward the curling wall of water waiting to swallow them. It was the most frightening thing she'd ever seen, so she didn't look at it, just closed her eyes, gritted her teeth, dug her left foot into the mushy sand and pulled with all her might.

The ocean was infinitely stronger, and though Cathy strained until her arms shuddered, it was a losing tug-of-war. Or so she thought until the undertow simply let go and the sudden release pitched her forward across Fin's back. Wrapping one arm around her waist, he came up running beneath her, slipping and falling but running nonetheless, as another white-capped breaker crashed ashore and surged up the beach in hot pursuit.

Bouncing across his shoulder, Cathy watched the wave churn toward them. She knew it would catch them, and it did, lassoing Fin and lifting him off his feet. Somehow he managed not to lose his grip on her as they bobbed along, choking and flailing, on the crest. When the breaker dropped them, the back of Cathy's head struck something hard, and Fin fell on top of her, knocking the wind out of her.

Gasping for air, she saw stars as the wave slid harmlessly away. Fin sprawled on his back and coughed while the frigid but gentler surf swirled them around, and rolled Cathy onto her stomach. Blinking through the seaweed stringing in her face, she looked at the driftwood tiger.

"This is all your fault," she panted, then collapsed.

4

SPRAWLED FACEDOWN on the wet, cold sand, Cathy savored being alive until another icy wave surged around her and nudged her a bit farther up the beach. Coughing saltwater, she picked up the tiger as Fin groped for her elbow and hauled her to her feet. She hadn't come this far to leave the saber-tooth behind.

Cradling it in the crook of her left elbow, she slipped her right arm around Fin's waist as he looped his left arm around her shoulders. Holding each other up, they staggered out of the surf with the rain pelting their backs and the wind snapping their soaked clothes.

Visibility was so poor that Cathy didn't see the step until she tripped over it, and the stumble she took brought them to a wavering halt. Peering through the soupy fog beginning to roll ashore behind the rain, she could just make out a flight of redwood stairs, a railed deck and the outline of an A-frame roof above it.

"Forget it," Fin said tiredly. "Nobody lives there."

"Under the c-c-circumstances," Cathy replied, her teeth chattering, "I'm not a-b-bove breaking in."

Swiping the rain out of his eyes with the back of his free hand, Fin looked up at the house. He seemed to be considering it, his chest rising and falling sharply beneath his sodden T-shirt, then abruptly shook his head as a chill caused him to shudder.

"Security system," he said. "Desperate as I suddenly am for a place to sleep, I'd prefer not to spend the night in the constable's jail."

Cathy could've cried but instead bit her lip as Fin tugged her away from the stairs. So wet and cold that her bones ached, she'd never felt this miserable in her life, not even while she'd been married to Garrett.

The rain began to slacken, but the fog was growing denser by the second, so dense they couldn't find the Jeep. After five minutes of wandering around in the milky gloom with Fin holding Cathy's hand and walking slightly ahead of her, he found it—by smacking face first into the passenger door.

The impact knocked him flat. He sat for a second, then grabbed the side mirror, pulled himself to his feet and threw his arms around Cathy.

"Eureka!" he cried and kissed her.

As cold and shivery as his mouth felt against hers, it was the best kiss she'd ever had. Maybe because she hadn't been kissed by a man since Garrett, but more than likely because they'd almost drowned and it felt so good to be alive. So good that Cathy flung her arms around Fin and kissed him back. Not with much style or finesse, but ardor enough to make him groan as he unwrapped her hands from the back of his neck and held them tightly in his.

"Remind me to throw myself in the surf daily."

"I will not."

"Then at least promise to kiss me once a day."

"On one condition."

"Name it."

"Get me the hell out of this rain."

"Done."

Fin opened the door, let Cathy scramble inside and slammed it behind her, shaking loose the raindrops clinging to the window. Hugging herself for warmth, she watched them run down the glass past the AMC/Jeep sticker pasted to the inside. She wondered why he lived in a hovel if he could afford a brand-new car?

She would've asked Fin about it as he swung himself in behind the wheel and turned the key dangling fortuitously from the ignition, but he switched on the dome light along with the engine and windshield wipers. Blinking in the sudden glare, Cathy looked down at the saber-toothed tiger lying on its back in her lap. Her breath caught in her throat, her eyes widened and she felt her neck tingle.

Old and scarred as the driftwood was, the three words burned into it along the tiger's belly were still legible. The *i* had worn almost completely away, but Cathy didn't need it to read the name *Rachel Simms*.

She'd spent half her girlhood looking for a piece of Captain Croft's ship, and now that she'd found one, she couldn't quite believe it, couldn't quite figure out what it signified. But it meant *something*; she was positive of that. It wasn't a thought so much as a feeling, a feeling as real as the cold chunk of driftwood in her lap, a feeling that made her heart pound with excitement and trepidation.

"I said are you all right, Cath?"

Startled by the nearness of Fin's voice, Cathy whirled toward him. He leaned on his right arm, his face so close to hers that the tiny grains of sand caked in his eyebrows glittered like diamonds.

"I—y-yes," she stammered.

"You sure?" He raised his left hand and gently grazed his cold and not quite steady fingertips along her hairline. "You're pale as death."

"I'm fine. Half-frozen, but fine."

"I can fix that."

Straightening behind the wheel, he switched on the heater and the defroster, and then the headlights. The beams shot across the beach, illuminating the roof of the cabin bobbing away on the roiling surf.

Fin swore softly. "I knew I should've replaced those rotten stilts."

Muttering under his breath, he shifted the engine into gear and turned the Jeep toward the road. The tires spun and spit sand, thunder boomed so loud and close by the windshield and dashboard vibrated. A vicious broadside slap of wind fishtailed the Jeep off the beach and onto the road, and made Cathy shiver.

"I'm sorry about your cabin."

"Not your fault," Fin replied, frowning as the Jeep hydroplaned through a low spot and seawater sprayed the undercarriage. "Wasn't much of a cabin anyway."

"Had the water ever come up that high before?"

"Never." He raised his right hand from the wheel and swept his hair off his forehead as the road and the Jeep climbed higher ground. "What a bloody freaky thing."

Maybe not so freaky, thought Cathy, watching wisps of fog skim past the windshield. It seemed to her that the pale fingerlike tendrils were clawing at the glass. And the wind tearing violently at the Jeep sounded like an outraged howl.

The sea never gave back what it took. Not unless it spat this tiny little piece of the *Rachel Simms* by accident and realizing its mistake came to fetch it home just as Cathy had for her grandmother.

"Finders keepers," she murmured, clutching the tiger protectively as she looked out the side window at the breakers still swelling and foaming and hurling themselves at the Vineyard. "It's mine now."

"What'd you say?" Fin asked.

"Nothing." Cathy smiled to cover the lie as she shifted around in her seat to face him.

It was a feeble effort, her mouth trembling along with the rest of her. Fin glanced at her, one eyebrow raised as he leaned forward and directed two of the vents at Cathy.

"I'm real, y'know. I thought we'd established that."

Not that again. She groaned silently, but said matter-of-factly, "Of course you are."

"Then why are you sitting over there looking like you're being carried off to hell by Bluebeard's ghost?"

"I'm not. I'm sitting over here freezing to death."

It was another lie. Hot air rolled full tilt out of the vents and sweat prickled in her scalp, but she'd rather die of heat prostration than say what she was thinking and risk him laughing at her again.

"Cath," he said, a curt I'm-losing-my-patience edge to his voice. "It's so bloody hot in this car my clothes are steaming."

"At least one of us is warm," she replied lamely.

"That same one of us is also trying to salvage this less than auspicious beginning of our acquaintance." He shot her a sideways frown. "And you're making it damn difficult."

Truthfully, she was making it impossible. Cathy knew she was, but short of confessing her fantastic ruminations she didn't know how to change it. And the more she considered it, the less certain she was that she wanted to. Fin McGraw lived like a pauper but drove a brand-new car. Her grandmother said he was a playwright; he said he was an actor.

Cathy had no idea *Who* was on first or *What* was on second. The only thing she knew for sure was that *I Don't Know* was hugging the bag tightly at third.

"It's been a rough day," she told him. "I've never been in a shipwreck before, let alone a cabin wreck."

"Come to think of it, neither have I," Fin said, smiling at her and relaxing his tight grip on the wheel. "Sorry. I'm being an ass."

"What d'you say we start over?" Cathy offered her right hand. "Cathy Martin, nice to meet you."

"Fin McGraw." He clasped her hand and smiled again. "Charmed."

"I think I'm warm enough."

"Thank you!" He turned the heater off, the left turn signal on and the Jeep off the road onto the driveway that led to Cat's House.

In the wash of the headlights, the salt grass lay sodden and limp against the flanks of the dunes. Muddy water filled ruts in the gravel and splashed over the hood and the windshield as the Jeep bounced to a stop near the front porch. Though Cathy figured it couldn't be much later than five or five-thirty, her grandmother's house lay dark beneath the almost night-black sky.

"Where d'you suppose Grandma's gone to in this storm?"

"Probably to bed with a flashlight," Fin replied. "The power almost always fails when it rains this hard."

Cat had a flashlight, but she hadn't gone to bed. She met them with it at the front door, the beam as bright and welcoming as a lighthouse beacon.

"Well, finally," she said. "Whatever took you so long to get here?"

Freshly drenched from running to the house from the Jeep, Cathy stood dripping on the porch with Fin and the tiger and stared at her grandmother.

"You've been expecting us?"

"But of course! That rat hole Phineas lives in leaks like a sieve!"

"Not anymore, Cat," he said, reaching ahead of Cathy to open the screen door. "That rat hole washed away."

"No!" she cried, backing away as Fin followed Cathy into the foyer.

"Yes," he replied as the screen door slapped shut and he closed the inside door behind them.

"Well, I'll be damned," Cat said.

The glaring halo cast by the flashlight obliterated her grandmother's face, but Cathy could hear the suppressed laughter in her voice.

"What's that in your hair?" Cat asked, shining the beam in her eyes.

"Seaweed," she answered, shielding her face with her right forearm. "We almost washed away with the rat hole."

"Since you found my tiger I'm awfully glad you didn't." The flashlight raked across the candlelit living room and came to rest on the mantel above the fireplace. "Put him there, then fetch a candle and I'll light your way to the bathroom. You smell like a salt cod, darling girl."

"Thanks, Grandma."

"Not to worry," Fin put in cheerfully. "I've always been particularly fond of salt cod."

Cathy ignored the comment, but Cat laughed. A bit too coquettishly, her granddaughter thought as she carried the saber-tooth across the living room and remembered the subtle-as-a-sledgehammer pass Fin had made at her. Her grandmother had indeed not lost her touch, and this was the first thing Cathy intended to discuss with her as soon as she could get Cat alone. The second thing was the tiger, which she placed gently, almost reverently, on the mantel between a pair of pewter candlesticks.

As she did, lightning forked just outside the windows, casting the room in eerie phosphorescence. In that half second of illumination, the candle flames seemed to shrink and the hollows in the face of the saber-tooth glowed like cat's eyes. Cathy froze, then nearly jumped as the thunder came, a monstrous crack that made the walls reverberate and the glass fire screen on the hearth tremble.

"Woo, close one," Fin said. "You may lose more than your lights, Cat."

"Since you've already offered up your cabin," she replied blithely, "I think my house is safe enough. The storm gods would be awfully greedy to demand a second sacrifice."

From the tone of her voice, Cat was clearly joking, but Cathy, still unnerved by the lifelike spark she'd seen in the tiger's face, shivered at the mention of gods and sacrifice. She backed haltingly away from the fireplace, telling herself her eyes were playing tricks in the dark.

As another long-fingered lightning bolt snaked past the window, Cathy snatched up a candle and scurried across the living room. When the thunder cracked a low, rumbling growl not nearly so close or fierce as the last, she was halfway up the stairs with Fin and Cat, her hand tucked safely in the curve of her grandmother's elbow.

5

CATHY HAD NEVER SHOWERED and washed her hair by candlelight before and hoped she'd never have to again. It was treacherous and scary, the smeary lick of the candle flame on the other side of the pebbled glass door uncannily like the glow she'd seen in the eyes of the driftwood tiger.

Thought she'd seen, Cathy corrected herself as she parked the candle on her dresser and groped through a suitcase for clean clothes. She had a splitting headache, she was shaken, confused and considered running home to Mommy and Daddy.

The impulse was one hundred percent pure cowardice and though it sounded good it felt wrong. As much sense as Had's "glassy eyed an' mumblin'" description of Cat's ex-coauthors was beginning to make, Cathy couldn't bail out on her grandmother and her memoirs—or herself.

She hadn't realized how easily she'd slipped back into her nonaggressive push-me-around-I-love-it behavior until the worst of her panic had gone down the drain with the mud, the sand and the seaweed. She knew she had to break the pattern and assert herself—especially with Cat—or go back to London in defeat.

Deciding she'd rather walk naked through Boston Common, Cathy dressed and figured out what else—besides the aberration with the saber-tooth—was bothering her. There were several things, she discovered, all of them pertaining to Fin McGraw.

In addition to the business about his Jeep and his shack, and whether he was an actor or a playwright, Cathy wanted to find out how long he'd known her grandmother and just exactly what their relationship was. Since she'd kissed him on the beach, she knew why she wanted to kick herself for rebuffing the pass he'd made at her, but beyond that she needed information. And aspirin.

So she brushed her towel-dried hair, held it back from her face with a red plastic headband, picked up her candle and headed downstairs in jeans and a gray sweatshirt. The storm was still blustering and rumbling discontentedly when she came into the living room, which was lit by numerous candles and the fire crackling behind the glass screen. Cat had changed the pink jogging suit she'd worn earlier for a white one, and was crawling on the carpet, spreading a blue gingham tablecloth.

"What's this for?" Cathy asked, dropping to her heels to straighten a corner her grandmother had missed.

"I thought we'd have supper here," Cat said with a smile. "Doesn't that sound like fun?"

"A real picnic."

While Cat laughed at her pun, Cathy walked to the fireplace. She stood nose to nose with the saber-tooth until her eyes burned from staring at the dripping candles wavering from the heat waves radiating through the screen. She kept waiting for the tiger to do something, but it just sat there between the pewter sticks, a lifeless chunk of driftwood carved by water, time and weather to look like a big cat drawn back on its haunches, jaws open, one gnarled paw raised.

Either it's playing possum or I really did imagine it, Cathy thought, afraid she'd imagined seeing *Rachel Simms* burned into the tiger's belly as well. Her fingers itched to turn the saber-tooth over and check, but she decided not to push her luck.

"Where's Fin?" she asked, turning toward Cat.

"Looking through Phineas's clothes for something to wear."

"I didn't know you'd kept any of Granddad's things."

"Just his favorites." Cat struck a fireplace match and lit a four-armed silver candelabra.

"You don't mind them being worn?"

"Why should *I* mind?" Cat looked at her askance and blew out the match. "You might ask Phineas if he minds, but I can't think why he would since he no longer wears them."

Cathy groaned, pinching the bridge of her nose as her headache flared. "Do you still keep aspirin in the kitchen?"

"In the cabinet next to the sink."

"I'll be right back."

At the sink Cathy washed down two caplets. A deep sigh fluttered out of Helmut's bedroom, the butler's pantry in Captain Croft's day. Remembering that he went to bed when it rained "t'ride it out" as he'd done in the merchant marine, she raised her candle and leaned around the wall separating the back hall from the kitchen.

A flare of lightning glared through the window above the sink and illuminated Helmut's sleeping form. Lying on his back, hands folded on his massive chest, he looked like a beached whale. Fiercely devoted to Cat, he thoroughly disliked everyone else in the northern hemisphere, if not the entire world.

Was it just his distaste for humanity in general, Cathy wondered, that prompted Helmut to call Fin "that bum what lives down the beach," or did he know something she didn't? She longed to ask him, yet knew from experience it would be useless. Helmut presided over Catherine

Lindsay's household like the silent and inscrutable Buddha he resembled.

Sighing, Cathy returned to the living room just as her grandmother lifted the wicker picnic hamper onto the cloth.

"I left that on the beach."

"I know. I saw you through my telescope. I sent Hadley for it once you'd gone."

"You were spying on me?"

"Of course." Cat opened the basket, took out two Spode dinner plates and a pair of Waterford champagne flutes. "We need another place setting, darling girl, and there's a tomato aspic in the fridge I suppose we should eat since heaven only knows when the lights will come on."

Doubling back to the kitchen, Cathy found the aspic and a bag of parsley with the aid of her candle, then collected another plate, goblet and silverware from the breakfront in the dining room. She left her candle there, balanced the aspic on top of the dishes and went back to the living room. Standing at the edge of the tablecloth, she frowned at her grandmother.

"What would you have done if I'd stayed behind the rocks with the hamper?"

"I'm sure I would've thought of something."

"Oh, I'm sure." Cathy set the aspic, the china, the crystal and the silver in front of her grandmother as she sat down. "I suppose I should have smelled a setup when you gave me the basket."

Cat arranged the plates and champagne flutes, then looked at her incredulously. "You didn't?"

"I was a bit rattled. After all your carrying-on about Phineas writing a play for me and Phineas admiring the tiger, you had me half-convinced I was going to meet Granddad."

Cat laid out the silverware and laughed. A bit hollowly, thought Cathy, watching the aspic quiver precariously as her grandmother picked it up and moved it in front of her.

"What an imagination," she said admiringly.

"It's not my imagination he looks like Granddad spit him."

"There's a resemblance, perhaps." Cat shrugged offhandedly and opened the bag of parsley.

"You told me he's a playwright, but he says he's an actor."

"What does *he* know?" Cat retorted, angrily stabbing the aspic with little green sprigs. "If he knew anything he'd do audiences everywhere a favor and get off the stage! Handsome as Apollo, yes, but as wooden as the sets."

"Is he or is he not a playwright, Grandma?"

"Let's just say he shows great promise."

"Which means?"

"Which means he has a certain flair for the dramatic. All Irishmen are born with the soul of a poet, it's in their blood. Unfortunately for Fin, his freezes on stage, so I've been—hmm, how best to say this?" Cat paused thoughtfully with a stalk of parsley pinched between each thumb and forefinger. "Exposing him to alternative forms of expression."

"Such as play-writing?"

"Why, yes." Cat smiled brightly. "We've been reading your grandfather's work Fin and I, and I must tell you, he has some marvelous ideas for structure—very fresh and innovative—and a great ear for dialogue. Not quite brilliant, not yet, but I feel we are very close."

"Does Fin agree with the career change you're planning for him?"

"I am not planning. Envisioning, yes. Visualizing and affirming it daily to manifest it on the physical plane, but *planning*—" Cat put aside the parsley and picked up her cigarettes and pink butane lighter. "Definitely *not*."

"But you did plan the rendezvous on the beach?"

"I thought we'd established that." Cat shook out a cigarette, put it in her mouth and impatiently flicked her lighter.

"And Fin was your willing accomplice?"

"Of course he was willing," she replied, the cigarette bobbing in the corner of her mouth as she lit it. "But my accomplice, *no*."

"Why didn't you just invite him to dinner?"

Cat snorted smoke disdainfully through her nostrils. "How pe*des*trian."

"How simple."

"Unimaginative," Cat countered, "and uninspired."

"But not convoluted or underhanded."

"Underhanded!" Cat sprinkled ash on the aspic as she plucked the cigarette from her lips. "I stage a romantic interlude worthy of Shakespeare, cast you opposite a handsome Celt, who you've always been such a sucker for! Not a pale impotent ass like—like—"

"Garrett," Cathy filled in.

"Like *Garrick*! But a man of passion and joie de vivre, and this—this accusation is the thanks I get!"

"We're talking about my life, Grandma, not a Broadway show," Cathy replied evenly. "Envision, visualize and affirm all you like, but don't send me off to any more assignations like a walk-on in the second act."

Counting to eight in her head, Cathy held her grandmother's blistering glare until Cat, her eyes narrowing suspiciously, shifted to reach the ashtray on the coffee table.

"You flubbed your lines, didn't you?"

Cathy sighed. "I blew them."

"Tell me what happened." Cat put out her cigarette and folded her hands in her lap.

Omitting her faint, her believing Fin was Phineas and the pass he'd made at her, Cathy gave her a blow-by-blow account of the wreck of his cabin and their escape up the beach. Because she didn't think it was important, she also left out the A-frame she'd stumbled over.

By the time she reached their wandering through the fog, she was on her feet, her commentary as animated as her pantomime of Fin holding on to her with one hand and groping his way through the gloom with the other. When she illustrated his face-first smack into the Jeep with a stage fall worthy of Chevy Chase, Cat threw back her head and laughed.

"What a marvelous gift of mimicry you have." Sighing, she plucked a lace-trimmed hankie from the cuff of her left sleeve and wiped her eyes. "I haven't laughed so hard since the sea gull pooped on Helmut's head."

"But he never goes out of the house!"

"And now you know why."

They both laughed then, until the storm loosed an ear-shattering barrage of wind and thunder that moaned through the eaves and shuddered the clapboard siding. A tearing *cr-rack* struck the east side of the house, startling Cathy and spinning her around to look. Sheet lightning flickered like a strobe outside the library windows, illuminating two shutters swinging free of their latches.

"I'll fasten them," Cathy said, getting to her feet.

"Don't bother," Cat replied as she moved toward the library. "We lose shutters willy-nilly in storms like this."

"But with the glass exposed—"

The storm cut her short with another volley that tore a third shutter off the long bank of windows facing the beach. This was why Cat always kept the shutters and the paneled doors that joined the library and the living room closed. Maybe twice in her life Cathy had seen them open, once when her father had gone into the library to look for a book. What in the world, she wondered, were the doors doing open in such a storm?

An exact replica of her grandfather's study in the New York apartment he and Cat had shared, she vaguely recalled the library was decorated like a minefield with Victorian monstrosities inherited from his mother. Stretching her arms out to feel her way across the room, she inched toward the windows while the wind repeatedly bashed the loose shutter against the glass.

"Darling girl!" Cat cried worriedly. "Come out of there at once!"

If she'd been able to move, Cathy would have, but she was frozen halfway across the room inhaling deep breaths of tobacco-scented air. It wasn't cigarette smoke, but pipe smoke, a tart, fruity blend. She'd only smelled it once, years ago, yet she recognized it instantly. Her father had bought a tin of it, but it had stirred so many memories for him he'd only been able to smoke one pipeful.

It was called Autumn Orchard, and it was the only tobacco Phineas Martin ever smoked.

6

NEON FLICKERS OF LIGHTNING illuminated the banging shutters. The rain pelting the windows was driven by a wind so fierce it didn't have a chance to run. Neither did Cathy, even though the smell had begun to fade.

It wasn't her imagination. The smell was still there, and so was the feeling of impossibility holding her in thrall.

How did I miss it, she wondered numbly, why didn't I see the rabbit hole I've fallen into?

"Hello, Cath, what the devil are you doing?"

Reality returned with the sound of Fin's voice. Cathy turned her head and looked at him leaning against the doorjamb behind her with a candle in one hand and a white meerschaum pipe in the other.

Without thinking, she whirled and grabbed it away from him. A microsecond before she raised it to her nose and inhaled stale, burned tobacco, she realized the pipe was cold, that it probably hadn't been within striking distance of a match since Harry Truman was president.

"Where did you get this?" Cathy demanded, pointing the meerschaum at him stem first.

"I found it in the pocket of these trousers." He snatched it back from her and frowned. "But I don't smoke tobacco or anything else anymore. I haven't since the night I found myself on the beach greased with vegetable shortening and ready to swim to the mainland."

"So you smell it, too."

"Smell what?"

"Smoke."

"Not yet." One corner of his mouth lifted crookedly as he took a step toward her. "But if we stand this close a bit longer I will."

"Will you two please come away from there! Go flirt where I don't have to worry you'll be impaled by flying glass!" Cat swept up beside them and grasped the library door handles. "Open the champagne, Fin, pour you and I a glass, then give the rest to my granddaughter—it'll help. Now *shoo!*"

He laughed, stopped as Cathy shot him an "I wouldn't" glare and trailed her soberly across the living room. As they sat down on opposite sides of the tablecloth, Cathy heard the library doors thud shut. She didn't hear the lock click, but glanced up at Cat just as she slipped the brass skeleton key into the breast pocket of her jogging suit.

"Now let's eat." Patting her concave bosom protectively, she came back to the tablecloth. "I'm famished!"

Cathy wondered why she locked the doors. To keep someone out, or someone *in*? It was crazy, insane—impossible—and her grandmother wasn't crazy. Certainly more outrageous than she remembered, perhaps slipping a bit, but not crazy.

Closing her eyes, she raised one hand to her splitting head. She had not imagined smelling Autumn Orchard any more than she'd imagined seeing her grandfather on the beach. There was a rational explanation for the pipe smoke, perhaps something as simple as mistaking Fin for Phineas. All she had to do was remain calm until she found it. There was no such thing as ghosts, there was only—

Her breath caught in her throat, her eyes sprang open and she looked at Fin, who grimaced as he worried the cork out of a bottle of Dom Perignon. There was only a man who looked like a ghost.

Which had absolutely nothing to do with her grandfather's pipe smoke, but everything to do with Cat's ex-coauthors. How many of them had seen Fin McGraw and been struck by his uncanny resemblance to Phineas Martin? Had they mentioned it to Cat and been shrugged off as she had? Oh, it was possible, and more than probable that Cat, who had a tendency to tell everything she knew, had in turn confided her metaphysical designs for Fin and his career. Oh, *yes*. It added up to more than enough to send the seven poor "fellers" running "glassy eyed an' mumblin'" for the ferry.

As for the pipe smoke, all she had to do was get the key away from her grandmother and investigate the library. Feeling smug and greatly relieved, Cathy offered her glass to Fin as the cork gave way with a mellow pop and a cloud of gas curled out of the bottle.

"Fill 'er up, please."

"My pleasure." Smiling with only one side of his mouth again, he rose on his knees to pour the wine.

Always the right side, Cathy noted. Her grandfather's white shirt, red suspenders and pin-striped gray trousers smelled faintly of moth balls; they also fit Fin as if they'd been made for him.

"Thank you," she said as he sat back on his heels and made a face.

"By the way..." Reaching behind him, he pulled the meerschaum out of his pocket.

"My God!" Cat gasped. "Where did you find that?"

"In the pocket of these trousers." Fin glanced up at Cathy and frowned perplexedly. "But it's not mine."

"This is Phineas's favorite pipe," Cat said softly as she took it away from him. "He'll be so pleased I've found it. I haven't seen it since the day he died. How odd that it's turned up now." She paused and gazed thoughtfully at Fin.

"But perhaps not. You know, I believe those are the clothes he was wearing that afternoon."

On cue, lightning flashed and thunder rumbled. Odd schmod, Cathy told herself bravely, shrugging despite the chill crawling up her back.

"Really?" Fin asked as he filled Cat's flute and then his own.

"Yes, I believe so. Red is his favorite color, you see, and he's especially fond of pinstripes. If I'm correct, there should be two or three buttons missing. I ripped them off pulling up his shirt after he'd fainted."

Fascinated, Cathy watched Fin put down the champagne bottle and loosen the shirt from the waistband of the trousers. Sure enough there were three empty buttonholes. She stared at them a moment, then drank her wine in one swallow. It went straight to her headache, made her temples throb miserably, but got rid of her chill.

"Silly, silly man," Cat murmured, tracing the carved bowl with her fingertips. "He got up from his chair, put his hand on his side and said, 'If this damned tick doesn't go away, I shall never finish the third act.' Then he fainted at my feet."

"Third act?" Cathy echoed. "What third act?"

Still gazing at the meerschaum, a distant, misty smile on her face, Cat didn't answer.

"The third act of the play he was writing when he died," Fin explained.

"What play? He and Grandma were touring Ireland when his appendix burst."

"I've read it," Fin said with a shrug. "It's not bad."

"Oh, yeah?" Cathy bristled. "How come I haven't?"

"For heaven's sake, darling girl," Cat snapped testily. "There's no need to be petulant. It's around here somewhere. I'll find it for you so you won't feel left out."

"Does my father know about this play?"

"I may have given it to him at the wake." Cat put down the pipe, picked up her cigarettes and lit one. "Things were such a mess with packing and red tape I frankly don't remember." She plucked her cigarette from her mouth and shuddered. "Never die in Ireland, darling girl."

"God knows that's why I left," Fin quipped.

He and Cat looked at each other and laughed. Cathy heard a faraway bell ring inside her head. Something about Ireland—or was it dying?—had set it clanging, but she couldn't quite remember what. Something she'd read someplace. . . .

"Now that you're an orphan of the storm," Cat said to Fin, loudly as if to gain Cathy's attention, "you will of course move in with us."

Cathy gaped at her grandmother, and so did Fin, his glass half raised to his mouth.

"Oh—right! No cabin." His uptake was so abrupt Cathy could almost hear the sudden click of a missing piece falling into place. "Sorry." He quaffed his wine and smiled. "I'm having such a good time I'd forgotten."

"Uh-huh," Cathy said slowly. "I can see how being homeless could slip your mind."

Fin laughed but shot Cat a furtive glance. Was it a guilty look, Cathy wondered, or was she imagining things again? She could've sworn he'd not only damn near blown his cue but his lines as well. If this were a fairy tale, she thought, I'd be Little Red Riding Hood. But in this version Grandma is in cahoots with the Big Bad Wolf.

The sixty-four-thousand-dollar question was why. What was there to conspire about? Fin's cabin had been swept out to sea; he had no place to go. Unless he wanted to sleep in his Jeep, the brand-new one, which, if his shack was any reflection of his checkbook balance, he couldn't afford. But her grandmother, with the tidy little fortune she'd made during her long career in the theater and movies along with the royalties from Phineas's plays, could afford a fleet of Jeeps.

The thought gave Cathy an uncomfortable twinge in her trust fund, but it was an inescapable possibility. Clearly Cat doted on Fin McGraw, and if he had even the tiniest bit of larceny in his heart, her grandmother would be easy pickings.

"I *said*, darling girl—" Cat waved one hand in front of her face "—would you care for some stuffed squab?"

Cathy started and blinked at the contents of the hamper that were now on the tablecloth.

"No, thank you. I'm not very hungry."

"Are you feeling well?" Cat laid a hand on her knee. "You usually eat like a horse."

"I'm fine, Grandma. Just tired."

"I'd be more than happy to take you to bed," Fin volunteered.

"I'm not *that* tired," Cathy snapped, but her grandmother laughed uproariously.

Shrugging good-naturedly, Fin tore a leg off the squab, wrapped the knuckle in a gingham napkin and offered it to Cat. She accepted it with a courtly nod, her sapphire eyes luminous in the glow of the candles.

"Why, thank you, kind sir."

"My pleasure, madam."

Don't be hasty, Cathy cautioned herself as she watched Fin smile fondly at her grandmother. Maybe that isn't avarice gleaming in his eyes, maybe it's only Dom Perignon.

By the time they'd polished off Helmut's sinful spread, eight o'clock had come and gone, chimed by the grandfather clock in the foyer. Except for occasional gusts of rain and wind, the storm had all but blown itself out. The champagne was almost gone, as were the candles, and the electricity was still off.

"I think it's safe to say—" Cat yawned "—that the power will not be restored this evening. And I, for one, vote for an early bed."

"Make that two," Fin said, smiling raffishly at Cathy.

"Make it one," she replied coolly. "My vote cancels your vote."

Once the remnants of the picnic were packed away in the hamper, Fin went up the stairs first, carrying the candelabra. Cathy followed, using a candle in a brass stick with her grandmother on her arm. The carpeted steps groaned beneath them and the half-burned tapers cast long, vague shadows on the gallery walls.

"You may have any bedroom you wish," Cat said to Fin as they stopped outside her door. "But I'm particularly fond of the Blue Room. It has a lovely view of the beach at first light, and I'll sleep so much better with you on one side of me and my darling girl on the other."

Oh, please, Cathy moaned silently just as Fin raised the candelabra and looked at her face.

"I'm not much for watching sunrises," he said with a smile. "Not by myself anyway, and I think your darling girl will sleep better if I'm at the other end of the hall."

There was no sarcasm or malice in his voice, yet Cathy felt stung as she watched Fin touch his fingertips to her grandmother's cheek and walk away. The warmth and light went with him, leaving her alone with Cat in the pale shadow of the single taper.

"Remind me to call Pamela in the morning," Cat said, opening the door and marching boldly into her dark bedroom.

"My mother? Why?" Cathy asked, scrambling ahead of her to put the candle on the nightstand.

"On the off chance it's escaped her notice, I intend to tell her she's raised a ninny."

Cat sat down on the cannonball four-poster, peeled off her white ballet slippers and threw them at her granddaughter. Cathy caught one in each hand, then jammed her clenched fists on her hips.

"If refusing to sleep with a man I barely know makes me a ninny, then so be it."

"Oh, bosh!" Cat fumed, pulling her flannel nightdress out from under her pillow. "He's handsome and virile and absolutely mad about you! What more do you need?"

"Consideration, understanding, respect—"

"Poppycock!" Her grandmother's wispy white hair stood on end as she yanked off the top of her jogging suit.

The key to the library doors fell out of the pocket and landed, gleaming dully in the candlelight, on the braided rug at her feet. Quickly Cathy knelt to put Cat's slippers by the nightstand and palmed the key in her right hand.

"You need passion, darling girl, the grander the better." Her grandmother caught her hand, the left one, as she stood. "You need to look into the eyes of the right man and realize that up until that moment you've been dead from the waist down."

"I did that already." Cathy surreptitiously tucked the key into her back pocket and picked up her grandmother's nightdress. "That's why I'm divorced."

"I said the *right* man." Cat raised her arms and let Cathy ease the gown over her head. "His name is Phineas McGraw and he's just down the hall. If you don't believe me, go look in his eyes and see for yourself."

"Maybe tomorrow."

"Not tomorrow, *now!*" Cat caught both her hands and held them tightly to her bosom. "Don't think, just look. What d'you suppose would've happened if Phineas and I had stopped looking at each other in Aunt Elvira's parlor and started thinking? Neither you nor I would be here, that's what!"

"I'm not you, Grandma." Cathy dropped a kiss on her grandmother's forehead, freed her hands and tugged off Cat's white fleece bottoms. "And Fin isn't Granddad, no matter how much he looks like him."

"Oh, that damned nonsense!" Cat swung her legs onto the bed and the covers over her knees. "His nose is similar, perhaps his forehead—"

"His eyes, his ears, his chin and his mouth," Cathy finished, leaning over her and kissing her soundly. "Shall I leave the candle?"

"Hardly." Cat scowled and folded her arms. "I've almost ninety years' practice finding the toilet in the dark."

"All right, then, good night." She picked up the candle, walked to the sitting room door and opened it. "I love you, Grandma."

"I love you, darling girl." As Cathy pulled the door shut behind her, Cat added in a stage whisper, "But I still think you're a ninny."

7

CATHY WENT TO HER ROOM, put the candle on the night table and collapsed on her bed. The trees outside her window had been studded with tiny new leaves that morning, but the storm had stripped them winter bare. The branches tapped the glass like impatient fingers. Get up, Cathy, they said. Take the key out of your pocket, go down to the library and snoop.

"Oh, leave me alone." She groaned, pressing the heels of her hands to her eyes.

Although she knew she had to, she didn't want to snoop. Her grandmother snooped, her grandmother schemed, her grandmother connived and machinated. Always with the best interests of those she plotted for at heart, of course. She used to be discreet about it, but there was nothing at all subtle in her efforts to entice Cathy into Fin McGraw's bed.

If allurement didn't work, she was capable of trickery. Caveman tactics couldn't be ruled out, either. But what Cathy couldn't figure out was the hard sell, the push, the contrivance of sending her after the tiger.

Based on the kiss he'd given her when they'd found his Jeep, she was pretty sure she could've fallen for Fin McGraw all by herself. But no, that was too simple. Cat thought it was more fun to meddle, to monkey and mix signals, to bamboozle her to the point she thought Fin was a gigolo.

No, she couldn't blame that on Cat; she'd already begun to wonder about him. If only he didn't have navy-blue eyes and that sexy-as-hell Irish accent. If only he hadn't been so kind to her when she fainted. If only he wasn't so funny and so gentle with Cat. Then it'd be so much easier to distrust and dislike him.

Cathy's headache flared and she rubbed her temples. Oh, to hell with it. For all she knew he could be a CIA mole or the damn tooth fairy. The only person Cathy knew for sure he wasn't was Phineas Martin. He just looked like him . . . and maybe that was the problem.

Since she'd wakened on the beach and seen him leaning over her, events had taken a sharp turn toward the weird. Or had they? Thinking he was her grandfather had been one hell of a jolt, and maybe she wasn't over it yet. Maybe she *was* imagining things because she was in shock.

It was the best explanation yet for seeing the glow in the eyes of the driftwood tiger and smelling her grandfather's pipe smoke. Nothing even remotely weird or supernatural about it.

The pain in her temples flared again and her head swam. The champagne, she decided, raising one hand to her forehead. Better not snoop with a fuzzy head, better go to bed and sleep it off.

The tree branches rapped the glass again as she picked up the candle and carried it to the dresser. Nice try, they said, but we know avoidance when we see it.

Cathy opened a suitcase and glared at the trees. "Butt out of this, will you?"

They did, lifting away from the window in a stiff gust of wind that seeped through the sash and made the candle flame gutter. The branches rattled like old bones against the eaves, while the tattered remnants of the storm clouds scudded away beneath the almost full moon.

Absolutely she was avoiding the library. After the day she'd had, anybody in their right mind would. Unfortunately going down there was the only way to prove whether she'd actually smelled Autumn Orchard or imagined it.

"Hi ho, hi ho, it's off to snoop I go," Cathy grumbled, pawing through her clothes in search of a pair of pajamas that matched.

A limb bumped the eaves, the wind moaned and something somewhere in the house went thump. Puzzled, she turned her head toward the door and listened.

Thump…thump…thump. Faint and erratic as the noise sounded, she decided it must be the loose shutter. Shrugging, she gave up trying to match blue silk to green, and put on a bottom, a top and a short kimono.

Th-thum-thump . . . th-thum-th-thump.

Now it sounded like Morse code. What the hell is that, Cathy wondered, frowning as she fished the library key out of her jeans and slipped it into the pocket of her kimono.

Thump…thump…th-thump…thump…thumimp.

The noise reverberated up the walls and through the floor, like an air pocket in an old pipe. Gooseflesh sprang on Cathy's arms, just as the candlewick burned into a pool of hot wax, smoked and went out.

"That's it!" Slamming the suitcase shut, she marched across the room and opened the door.

She heard the noise again as she stalked down the gallery, and paused to listen.

T-tap . . . tap . . . t-t-tap. Now it sounded like hammer strikes, not thumps. Her closed door must have muffled the eerie sound coming from downstairs. It stopped as Cathy reached the landing.

She did, too, one hand on the banister as she waited. The dark shapes of the table, the harp-backed chairs, the quarterdeck rail and the living room lamp shades were outlined by the moonlight streaming through the lead-glass window above and behind her. Another gust of wind rattled the latch on the dining room French doors and set off a round of creaks and moans.

Cathy shivered, from cold, not fright. She'd stopped being afraid of the dark in first grade, and with the exception of the library and Helmut's bedroom, she knew every inch of Cat's House like the back of her hand.

Tap . . . tap . . . ta-ta-tap . . . tap.

It *was* a hammer, the strikes light and random. They echoed faintly as Cathy started down the bottom flight of steps and turned her head to get a fix on the direction. It almost sounded like somebody taking a sounding and—

Ta-ta-ta-tap . . . tap.

It was coming from the library. Either Had was nailing up the loose shutter in the dark or the brownies had picked a lousy goddamn time to come and fix the shoes.

At the end of her patience, and her credulity, Cathy bolted down the stairs. She found the candle she'd left on the breakfront, her grandmother's lighter on the table-cloth where she'd left it with her cigarettes and beside it the flashlight.

She grabbed the flashlight and switched it on, dropped the lighter in her pocket, took out the key, hurried across the living room and unlocked the library doors. One at a time she pushed them open, stepped into the room and drew a deep breath. She smelled stale, dusty air, but no pipe smoke.

And the tapping had stopped again.

Frowning, she pointed the flashlight at the windows. The unlatched shutter hung half-open but unmoving, even though the wind was still blowing and gusting fiercely. Of course it wasn't moving, she realized, the wind had switched when the storm ended. She'd ruled out the shutter. That left the stinking little fairies.

"Come out, come out, wherever you are," Cathy muttered, making a slow sweep of the room with the flashlight.

She didn't see any elves or brownies, not that it would have surprised her, just ornate tables cluttered with bric-a-brac, a brocade love seat, a chair and footstool and a hideous clubfooted desk the size of a billiard table. A hurricane lamp sat on one corner of it, the oil in its ruby-red base gleaming in the flashlight beam. Cathy took off the globe and lit the wick with her grandmother's lighter.

The lamp sputtered but finally caught, spreading a pool of light to warm the chilly shadows. Cathy shut off the flashlight and cringed. The library was, just as she'd remembered, the ugliest room she'd ever seen.

The desktop was the least cluttered surface in the room. There was only the lamp on one end, now emitting a curl of black kerosene smoke, and on the other end a rack full of pipes and a red leather humidor. The pleated green valance above the shutters looked gray with dust, as did the books on the shelves flanking the portrait of her grandfather on the wall behind the desk.

Cathy glanced briefly at the painting, then leaned against the front of the desk and waited. She'd counted nearly two hundred patient ticks of the grandfather clock before she realized she was not going to hear the tapping sound again.

It made no sense, yet Cathy couldn't shake the feeling she'd heard something she wasn't supposed to, that she'd interrupted something. Or someone. The only person in the house besides her and Cat and Helmut was Fin, but she refused to consider him. People in shock shouldn't make rash judgments.

Sighing, she turned around, picked up the humidor and tried to open it. The lid was on crooked, stuck as if it had been jammed on in haste, but finally came off in Cathy's left hand with a tinny pop and a puff of air redolent with the aroma of Autumn Orchard. The tobacco was fresh and moist, but it wasn't what she'd smelled earlier. She'd smelled smoke. Cathy replaced the lid and frowned. Why did her grandmother keep fresh tobacco for a dead man?

It was strange, but it hardly justified locking the doors. Nothing else she'd seen in the library did, either. Cathy gave the pipe rack an idle spin, thinking as she trailed her right index finger along the wobbling pipes.

She was about to lift her hand away when the white meerschaum she'd last seen in her grandmother's possession after she'd locked the library doors came around and stopped beneath her finger. The pipe was warm, the embers in the carved bowl glowing and drifting smoke.

This time she hadn't fallen down the rabbit hole, this time she'd stepped into the Twilight Zone. But she wasn't staying. She was getting the hell out—out of the library, out of this house and off the island.

Snatching her hand away, Cathy backed toward the door. The smoke rising from the pipe flattened and snaked after her, hooking back on itself like a beckoning skeletal finger. She froze. The smoke stopped, too, hovering, wafting, waiting. She sidled to the right and backed three more paces. The smoke wavered, curled, then followed.

Mewling with fright, Cathy edged toward the door. Her ears were ringing, her heart pounding. With her right hand, she groped behind her for the door handle, the molding—

Her knuckles brushed something warm, something warm that moved. Shrieking, she whirled, saw her grandfather standing behind her, then nothing but a kaleidoscopic blur of doorway, floor and ceiling.

When she came to with an eye-opening jerk, she was lying on the love seat, with a wet washcloth on her forehead. Fin sat beside her on the footstool, the red suspenders looped over his bare shoulders, his elbows bent on his knees and his fingers laced loosely together.

"Oh, God, not again." Cathy groaned, sliding the cloth over her eyes.

"'Fraid so. I caught you before you hit the floor, but you've got a bump on the back of your head."

"I know. I landed on Grandma's tiger on the beach."

"How d'you feel?"

"Foolish. Believe it or not, until today I've only fainted once in my life—on my wedding night."

Fin laughed. Cathy took the cloth off her head and glanced nervously toward the desk. The smoke had completely dissipated.

"You're pale as death. What happened?"

"I'd tell you but I'm not real sure myself. I don't even know where to begin."

"Start with what you were doing down here."

Cathy wasn't sure baring her soul to Fin was such a hot idea, but she felt the same compulsion to confess that had prompted her to tell Cat about seeing the ghostly Phineas on the beach.

"I heard noises."

"So did I. Sort of a bang."

"I thought it was a tap, like a hammer."

"Could've been. Then what?"

"Take a look at the pipe rack."

As Fin stood, straightening his long, muscle-rippled torso, Cathy's mouth went dry. She swallowed hard and watched him walk away from her. His back was as gorgeous as his chest. For thirty seconds or so he just stood beside the desk studying the pipes, then shot her a wary, sidelong glance.

"If this is a joke, I don't think it's funny."

"It's not a joke." Cathy swung her legs to the floor and sat up. "I found it there, lit and smoking. Furthermore, Grandma locked the library and put the key in her pocket before you gave her the pipe."

"If the doors were locked, how'd you get in here?"

"I filched the key from her."

Fin picked up the meerschaum and rubbed the bowl with his thumb.

"It's warm." He frowned and put it back in the rack. "And a lighter fell out of your pocket when you fainted."

"Wait a minute—"

"I think you staged this to get even with me for scaring you on the beach." He folded his arms and leaned against the desk. "But it wasn't necessary. You've made it clear you don't much care for me."

He had it all wrong, but Cathy wasn't sure she could explain it and make it right. She wasn't even sure there was a right, let alone a sensible or a rational explanation. Sighing, she raised a hand to her splitting head.

"I knew I should've kept my mouth shut."

"I'm sorry everything's gone so wrong. I told Cat the beach thing was a lousy idea, but she told me you had a great sense of humor and we'd all have a laugh."

"I do have a sense of humor, it's just—" Cathy stopped and considered what she was about to say. The truth couldn't mess things up any worse. "It's your face."

Fin gazed at her blankly, then cocked his head puzzledly. "What's wrong with it?"

"Look at the painting behind you."

He did, turning his head over his right shoulder.

"That's your grandfather."

"It could be you."

Fin glanced back at Cathy and raised one eyebrow.

"How hard did you hit your head?"

"Would you just take a good look at it?"

"I think you should." With his arms still folded, he walked around the desk and stood next to the portrait. "Over here where the light's better."

Why had she started this? Sighing, Cathy walked across the library and stopped in front of Fin. The light was much better. Strong enough that she could see her pajama bottoms were blue, her top green and her kimono pink. She looked like Cyndi Lauper. Fin gave her ensemble the once-over and smiled.

"I dressed in the dark," Cathy retorted defensively.

"I have the same color hair and the same color eyes as your grandfather, but that's about it. Have a look."

Seeing the portrait up close, she realized the shape of Fin's nose was different; it was longer, his nostrils more tapered. His cheekbones were higher, his jaw not as square as her grandfather's.

"The artist took a lot of license," she said stubbornly. "I think a photograph would be a fairer comparison."

"I also have the same first name. You've had a nasty crack on the head and—" His eyes widened incredulously. "You thought I was him, didn't you?"

Cathy tried to stonewall again, but it didn't work.

"That's what all this nonsense is, isn't it?"

"It isn't nonsense, it's—"

"You're right, it's insanity."

Fin tried to sidestep her and reach the door, but Cathy grabbed the flashlight off the desk and brandished it.

"Hold it right there, buster."

"I've heard enough of this, Cath. I'm going to bed."

"So am I, but not by myself." She switched on the flashlight. "Turn off the lamp."

Fin crossed his arms and glowered. "A simple please will do. You needn't threaten me."

Cathy glanced at the flashlight, cocked in both hands above her right shoulder like a Louisville Slugger. What was she doing?

"I—I'm sorry," she stammered, lowering her arms. "I'm not a violent person. I just don't want to be left down here alone."

"You won't be." He reached across the desk and picked up the hurricane lamp. "Ladies first."

Feeling five years old and two inches high, yet grateful for Fin and the lamp at her back, Cathy turned and walked out of the library. She left the flashlight on, even though he followed her all the way to her bedroom.

"Thank you." Cathy turned to face him in the open doorway. In the smoky flicker of the lamp his handsome face was all angles and hollows. "I don't suppose you'd reconsider the Blue Room, would you?"

Fin shook his head. "I think I'll sleep better at the end of the hall."

8

CATHY LIT WHAT REMAINED of the candle in the brass stick, hid under the covers and tried not to tremble. Something very weird was going on around here. She didn't know what, why or how . . . and she no longer cared.

She was through trying to rationalize irrational happenings. That had come to a screeching halt with the come-hither pipe smoke in the library. Just as soon as the sun came up and she had light enough to get her suitcases into the car, she was going to run like hell for Boston.

Only she couldn't go there, Cathy realized, not without endless remonstrations and questions from her parents that she had no intention of answering. Thanks to Fin McGraw she'd had a taste of what telling the truth would get her—a quick trip to the nearest psychiatrist.

She'd go to New York instead, check into the Plaza and shop until she dropped. Surely Saks would help her forget about ghosts and pipes that somehow found their way through locked doors. What she needed was a plausible excuse for leaving, but she quailed at the thought of trying to lie to Cat.

Her grandmother wouldn't likely believe a forgotten dental appointment in London, or a sick friend. In the midst of trying to plot her escape, which included visions of her lowering herself and her luggage out the window with a rope made of bedsheets, Cathy fell asleep.

The muffled slam of a door and the burst of an engine woke her with a start. Bright sunlight streamed through the window. Throwing off the covers, she leaped to her feet and staggered as her forgotten headache exploded like a grenade. Her stomach lurched, but she gritted her teeth and made it to the north-facing window in the sitting room without throwing up. Through the half-open shutter, she saw Fin behind the wheel of his Jeep, watched him stretch his right arm along the top of the passenger seat above Cat's head and back the mud-spattered vehicle toward the road.

Yippee. Here was her chance to escape.

When the Jeep cleared the driveway and turned toward Edgartown, Cathy crept back to her bedroom, closed the shutters, put on her sunglasses and dug the last two over-the-counter codeine tablets out of the tin she'd bought at the chemist shop near her London flat. She swallowed them with half a glass of water in the bathroom, raised her shades and peered at her face in the mirror.

She had a matched set of bags under her eyes, and her recently permed hair was a frizzy mess, but she didn't have time to fix it. Fin and Cat could be gone all day—then again, they could be back in twenty minutes.

Opening the vanity drawer, Cathy rummaged through it for the blue banana clip she'd put there yesterday. It seemed more like two weeks ago, but she refused to think about that or the fact that this was the third failure of her assertiveness training in the past twenty-four hours.

Failure, hell, it was a complete breakdown. She was running away. Cathy knew she was, but couldn't face it. Maybe in the safety of Saks lingerie department, but not now. Wincing at the twinge of pain, she fastened the clip in her hair, hurried into her room and dropped to her knees to pull her still-packed suitcases out from under the bed.

She saw *Phineas's Rainbow* still stuck on its spine between the headboard and the wall where she'd thrown it the day before, fished it out and sat back on her heels to look at her grandfather's picture. Fin did have Phineas Martin's nose and his chin. The jawline was still off, but, goddammit, she was right. Close enough anyway. Just wait until he saw this.

What a coup de grace, what a perfect parting shot, even though she wouldn't be here to see it. She'd leave it in his room with an "I told you so" note. He deserved it, the arrogant jerk. How dare Fin tell her *he* would sleep better at the end of the hall?

Ten minutes later Cathy was dressed in jeans and a red striped sweater, with the few clothes she'd unpacked stuffed in her suitcases. It took her three trips to huff and puff them down the stairs and out of the house, gritting her teeth against her splitting head and queasy stomach.

Though Helmut rarely left his room between eleven and four, she played it safe and carried everything through the dining room, out the French doors and down the veranda steps. She didn't take time to strap them onto the luggage rack, either, just threw them into the back seat of the MG, then made one last dash into the house.

Her head and her heart pounding, Cathy ducked into the kitchen, tore a note off the magnetized pad on the fridge, then paused in the doorway. Mozart drifted out of Helmut's room, his morris chair creaked and paper crackled as he turned a newspaper or magazine page. So far so good. Taking the stairs two at a time, she let herself into Fin's bedroom with the book and a pen snatched off the breakfront.

The cannonball bed looked like a war zone, the pillows mashed against the headboard and the fitted yellow bottom sheet loosed from the corners of the mattress. The nightstand and the painted china lamp were sprinkled with ash, and an empty pack of her grandmother's cigarettes lay twisted beside an overflowing ashtray.

The smell of stale nicotine made Cathy's head thud, her mouth water and her bottom lip catch between her teeth. She hadn't seen Fin so much as glance at a cigarette, yet during the night he'd smoked at least a dozen of them right down to the filter. Obviously he hadn't slept at all at the end of the hall.

The wrecked bed and cigarette butts put a new slant on things. Cathy no longer felt vindictive. She felt confused, somehow responsible for his sleepless night, and like a thief being in his bedroom. She decided to leave the note on the dining room table instead.

The grandfather clock chimed eleven-thirty as she rounded the landing and dived down the last flight of steps. She laid the book on the table, pasted the note to her grandfather's collar, wrote, "Take a good *long* look," jotted her initials, tossed the pen on the breakfront, wheeled toward the French doors—and froze as the doorbell rang.

"Get that, would ya, Cath?" Helmut called.

Rats, she thought, "Sure," she answered. The bell rang again as she crossed the living room. Was fate cruel enough to throw an Avon lady in her path? Or a Jehovah's Witness? Nothing could be worse, she thought, until she entered the foyer and saw Noel Penney, "glassy eyed and mumblin' and goosier than the whole lot of 'em" Noel Penney, peering at her through the screen door.

"Cathy!" he cried happily and pulled the door open. *Oh, no.* She groaned. "Oh, Noel—what a surprise," she said as he stepped into the house and hugged her.

Since he lived in New York City, the chances were slim and none Noel had just happened into the neighborhood and stopped by to say hello. And since Cat wasn't here and she was, Cathy realized she was stuck with entertaining him until Cat returned. Inches, she thought longingly, she'd been only inches from a clean getaway.

Noel backed away from her and smiled. "You look great."

Baloney. She knew she looked as if she hadn't slept in weeks.

Noel's dark hair was grayer than she remembered, almost silver at the temples, and the laugh lines at the corners of his brown eyes were etched much deeper. He looked distinguished and dashing, like Omar Shariff sans a mustache, but, the way he held his mouth as he studied her face gave him a preoccupied, perhaps even troubled expression.

"On second thought, you look like hell. Are you feeling all right?"

"Well, I—" Cathy began, but got no further.

A sudden wave of nausea rolled up from her stomach and sent her lurching, one hand clapped over her mouth, for the downstairs bathroom. She made it, just barely, and hung over the toilet until her stomach had emptied itself. Then she flushed, washed her hands and face, rinsed her mouth with mouthwash and opened the door to find Noel hovering in the short hallway between the dining room and bathroom.

"Better?" he asked solicitously.

"Much." Cathy sagged against the doorframe with a wan smile. "I should've known better than to take codeine on an empty stomach, but this damn headache won't go away."

Noel tugged her hand away as she raised it to her head, backed her into the bathroom, flipped the wall switch and turned her face toward the light over the sink. The glare made Cathy wince and her temples pulsed sickeningly.

"How long have you had this damn headache?"

"Since yesterday when I whacked my head on a chunk of driftwood on the beach."

"Your pupils aren't focusing together," Noel told her. "Give me your car keys."

Cathy did, and an hour later found herself on an examination table in an Edgartown clinic listening to a thin, middle-aged doctor tell her she'd suffered a mild concussion. The worst was past, but she should take it easy for a couple of days. The doctor gave her painkillers for the headache and suppositories if the nausea reoccurred. With a grin on her face, she left the examination room and cheerfully told Noel the diagnosis.

"Since when is a concussion cause for celebration?" he asked, cocking a dubious eyebrow at her happy expression.

"Since it explains a couple of weird things that happened yesterday," Cathy replied as they walked to the car. While the concussion explained the optical illusions—the eerie glow in the eyes of the driftwood tiger and the snake charmer's dance performed by the pipe smoke—she refused to wonder how the meerschaum got into the library or the noises that Fin had heard, too.

Noel gave her a slow, sidelong look as they got into the MG. "What weird things?" he asked.

Again Cathy felt the compulsion to spill her guts, but this time managed to resist it. "Nothing, really. Just stupid little things." She shrugged and tugged a strand of hair that had escaped the banana clip away from her mouth. "The doctor said it was fairly normal after a crack on the head to see things that really aren't there."

Noel opened his mouth, then abruptly shut it, started the MG and backed it out of its parking space. Closing her eyes, Cathy leaned against the headrest and gave thanks for the concussion—and Noel, who'd come along in the nick of time to save her from her Chicken Little impulses.

Too bad the possibility of a concussion hadn't occurred to her before she'd made a complete ass of herself with Fin, she thought and then reminded herself she was here to help Cat write her memoirs, not to have an affair with a heart-breakingly handsome Black Irishman. What a crying shame that was, Cathy thought wistfully, opening her eyes as Noel turned the MG off the road and up the driveway.

Some of the deeper ruts were still puddled with rain, but the salt grass had recovered and rippled along the flanks of the dunes beneath a gusty breeze and bleached white clouds. Even the bilge-water-gray Atlantic looked clean—well, cleaner—and deceptively docile lapping at the beach at the end of the boardwalk.

The greenhouse door was propped open by a chunk of broken cement block, which meant Had was tending to business. The leaf buds stripped from the trees littered the drive and squished underfoot as Cathy and Noel got out of the MG, and he eyed her jumbled suitcases in the back seat.

"Want me to give you a hand with these?"

"Uh—yes, thanks." Cathy smiled to cover the guilty start she'd made. "I—uh—didn't have time to get them into the house yesterday."

"Tell me." He grinned and grunted as he tugged the two largest cases out of the car. "Where is Cat, by the way?"

"I don't know," she replied, leading the way up the veranda steps to avoid Helmut. "She and Fin were just leaving when I got up."

"Fin who?"

"McGraw. He lives down the beach. Or did, until his shack blew away in the storm we had yesterday."

"Must've been some storm."

"It was," Cathy replied feelingly, going inside first and holding the French doors open for Noel.

He turned sideways to pass her and put the cases down at the foot of the stairs. Cathy shut the door behind him and paused with her hand on the latch. The blue gingham tablecloth and the wicker hamper had been cleared away, but the library doors stood open as she and Fin had left them. Squelching the recollection of her grandfather's red suspenders against Fin's gorgeous chest and back, she rounded the quarterdeck rail and crossed the living room.

There was one last thing she wanted to make sure she hadn't imagined and stood for a moment before the fireplace just looking at the driftwood tiger. Be there, please be there, Cathy prayed, turning the saber-tooth over as she lifted it off the mantel. The *Rachel Simms*, sans the *i* just as it had been yesterday, was still burned into the tiger's belly.

Sighing away the last of her unease with the breath she hadn't been aware she'd drawn and held, Cathy smiled and felt oddly at peace. So what if Cat kept fresh tobacco for a dead man? So what if the white meerschaum found its way through locked doors? What difference did it make so long as she had the tiger?

"What's that, Cathy?"

"What I hit my head on," she answered, deciding it was all Noel, or anyone else for that matter, needed to know.

Replacing the tiger between the pewter candlesticks, she turned away from the mantel and saw Helmut looming in the kitchen doorway like a sumo wrestler braced for a match, a sour look on his face as he eyed Noel and her suitcases.

"So you're quittin' the ol' lady, too, huh?"

"Who me?" Cathy gave a hollow laugh. "Don't be silly. I left those in the car, that's all."

He rumbled something unintelligible and shifted his bulk around to glower at Noel. "You stayin' fer supper?"

"He's staying," Cathy blurted.

Hands on his hips, Noel raised a puzzled eyebrow at her while Helmut, still rumbling like a bull walrus, heaved himself back into the kitchen.

"Cathy—" Noel started toward her, but stopped as his gaze caught on the note stuck to *Phineas's Rainbow*.

Before she could stop him, he picked the book up from the table, read the note and peeled it off. He studied Phineas's picture for a moment, then eyed her quizzically. "What is this?"

"A long story," Cathy said with a sigh.

Noel put the book back on the table and his hands back on his hips. "You were leaving, weren't you?"

"That's ridiculous!" she lied hotly.

"Is it? Then why did you leave this note for Cat?"

"I didn't leave it for Grandma. I left it for Fin."

"What's it mean—'take a good long look'?"

Cathy realized the only way out of this was the truth. "We had a disagreement about his resemblance to Granddad. I said he looked like the portrait in the library, Fin said he didn't. I said a photograph would be a better comparison—"

"Does he?"

"God, yes! Plus his name is Phineas—Fin is a nickname. In the photo the resemblance is even stronger, so—"

"That's it! That explains everything!" A grin spread across Noel's face, but abruptly twisted into a puckered frown. "Well, no, not everything," he went on, his eyes drifting pensively toward the open library doors. "It explains why Cat speaks of Phineas in the present tense, which unnerved even me once or twice. That should shut Evan up, but it still leaves the noises Claude heard. . . ."

Cathy pounced on that. "What noises?"

"This is how he described them: 'While I nodded, nearly napping, suddenly there came a tapping, As of someone gently rapping, rapping at my chamber door.'" Noel pulled his gaze away from the library, with difficulty, it seemed to Cathy, and shrugged. "But you know what a nervous Nellie Claude is."

What Cathy knew was that last night she'd heard the same tapping. She'd hoped it was fairies; Claude thought it was Edgar Allen Poe's raven. Noel's description of him was apt, but Claude Nivens, a friend of her father's and, along with Evan Knowles, one of Cat's ex-coauthors, was one of the most sensible, pragmatic men she'd ever met.

"What are you trying to tell me, Noel?"

"I swore I wasn't going to tell you anything." He sighed and ran one hand through his hair. "I promised myself I was just going to give you my notes and my first draft and beat it out of here on the next ferry."

"'Glassy eyed an' mumblin','" Cathy said, noting his gaze had drifted again, somewhat vacantly, toward the library.

"What?" Noel glanced at her, his hand cupping the back of his head.

"That's how Had said you left here. 'Glassy eyed an' mumblin',' and 'goosier than the whole lot of 'em,' referring, of course, to Evan and Claude and Ham and Drew, and the rest of Grandma's ex-collaborators."

"Nice phrase." Noel rubbed his neck and smiled wryly. "Maybe Archer should ghost Cat's memoirs. If that old fart isn't a spook, I've never seen one."

"Spook! What's that supposed to mean? Had is . . ."

The rest of the sentence died on her lips, for she suddenly knew precisely what Noel meant. She'd thought Fin was a ghost herself.

"Lemme get this straight. Are you telling me Evan and Claude think Cat's House is haunted?"

Noel nodded slowly. Twice.

"Ham and Drew?"

He nodded again.

"And Barry and Skip and Lyle?"

Another nod.

"And Noel?"

"I wondered if Cat was exhibiting the early stages of Alzheimer's, perhaps, or—"

"*Noel!*" Cathy cried, aghast, even though she'd fleetingly entertained the same thought.

"It seemed a more reasonable explanation than to simply think she'd dropped both her oars, or that she believes the house is haunted, too."

"That's idiotic!" Cathy started indignantly toward him, but came to an abrupt halt as she remembered the humidor full of tobacco. "Oh, no. I wonder if one of the others found the Autumn Orchard?"

Noel eyed her puzzledly. "What's Phineas's pipe tobacco got to do with this?"

"There's a fresh tin of it in the library."

The look on his face, part astonishment and part horror, made Cathy bristle and wish she'd kept her mouth shut.

"Now look here, Noel. Grandma has kept a lot of Granddad's things. All the stuff in the library, some of his clothes—"

"I'm on your side, honey." He closed the gap between them and laid his hands on her shoulders. "I love Cat and I absolutely hate what's being said about her. I've done what I can to squelch it, but if those weird tales keep up and find their way into one of the gossip columns—"

"Enough said." Cathy put up a hand to stop him. "I remember how much it hurt to read about Garrett's latest fling on the front page of the *National Tattler*."

Noel cringed. "God forbid they get hold of the story."

A muffled slam, followed by a trill of Cat's trademark laughter, drifted through the foyer into the living room.

"They're back." Cathy gripped Noel's wrists imploringly. "You've got to stay and tell me the rest of this. Maybe I should call Dad and—"

"Don't bother. I stopped to see Lindsay on my way up here, tried again to get him to listen to me and he all but threw me out of the house."

"What do you mean 'again'?"

"I talked to him about a month ago, told him what Claude and Evan and Ham and Drew were saying, but he turned a deaf ear."

The screen door whapped shut, startling Noel and Cathy. Cat, with shopping bags draped over her arms, paused in midstep just inside the living room. Fin stopped in the doorway behind her, loaded like a pack mule with more bags and shoe boxes under his arms.

"Don't let us interrupt," Cat said coyly. "Please *do* carry on."

"Yes, do," Fin agreed.

Her grandmother was kidding, but the wry, so-that's-the-way-it-is twist to his mouth plainly said Fin wasn't. The thought that he might be jealous gave Cathy a thrill of hope.

"We were just talking," she said.

"Don't be shy, admit it." Noel gave her a wink and a quick squeeze and walked toward Cat. "We were necking."

Cat laughed, opened her arms and flung them, packages and all, around Noel. The string handles tangled and knotted, trapping him in her embrace. While they laughed and tried to undo the cat's cradle holding him captive, Cathy sidled up to the table, snatched up the note, crumpled it and stuffed it in her back pocket.

"Hold still," Fin ordered as he dropped his packages with a thud, stepped around Cat and reached for the snarled handles. His shoulder bumped the red fishnet carryall she favored more than a purse, spilling its contents, including a rolled newspaper, onto the floor. The tabloid unfurled as it fell, fanning out like a deck of cards, and came to rest right side up facing Cathy.

It was the latest issue of the *National Tattler*, and the king-size boldface headline read: Actress's Island Mansion Haunted by Ghost.

9

FOR HALF A SECOND Cathy stared at the headline, then she went down on her heels to grab up the *Tattler* before Noel, who'd disentangled himself from Cat, turned around and saw it. But as her fingers closed on the bottom edge, Fin's hand clamped like a vice on the top.

"Let go," Cathy whispered.

"No. I had it first."

"This is all your fault. You and your goddamn face."

"Oh, it's my goddamn face today, is it? Last night it was your grandfather's."

"I said, *let go*." She gritted her teeth, clenched the *Tattler* in both hands and tried to wrest it away from him.

Fin gave a mighty yank that not only ripped the paper out of her grasp but pulled them both off balance. They landed nose to nose glaring at each other, Fin on his tailbone and Cathy between his legs, her left knee coming down on his right thigh only a scant half inch from his fly. He gasped and so did she.

"Now see what you've done!" Cat exclaimed. Her neck chains dangled in front of Cathy's eyes as she bent and plucked the crumpled *Tattler* from Fin's crotch. "I shall have to buy another copy to put in my scrapbook." An Egyptian ankh clunked Cathy on the nose as her grandmother straightened and turned away.

"Scrapbook!" Her eyes flew up to meet Noel's equally startled gaze. They gaped at each other, then he sprang forward, lifted her off the floor and offered Fin a hand.

"Noel Penney. Going up?"

"Thanks. Fin McGraw," he said and nimbly levered himself to his feet.

They eyed each other, sizing one another up, then followed Cathy into the dining room, where Cat stood at the table trying to smooth the wrinkled *Tattler*.

"Why d'you want this garbage in your scrapbook, Grandma?"

"Oh, but it's marvelous garbage, don't you think?"

"No. I think it's vicious and libelous garbage."

Cat smiled slyly, her ink-smudged palms spread on the front page. "Only if it's untrue."

"This is nothing to joke about, Grandma. Your reputation is at stake!"

"Oh, pooh!" Cat picked up *Phineas's Rainbow*, slammed it down on the *Tattler* to hold it flat and glared at Cathy. "If my reputation can weather being called 'Lindsay the whore' because I fell in love with a married man, I think it will survive this!"

"But, Grandma, this makes you sound—"

"Crazy?" Cat challenged bitingly. "Then bully! Only think how many copies of my memoirs it will sell! They'll line up for blocks to buy the book about the nutty old dame with the ghost under her bed!"

Not to mention under her nose, Cathy thought, frowning at Fin. He was reading the story accompanying the headline over Cat's shoulder, a grin on his face as he nudged *Phineas's Rainbow* aside. The book lay back cover up, and though Fin was oblivious to her grandfather smiling up at him, Noel wasn't. He raised his eyes from the photograph, looked at Fin, then at Cathy with a slow nod.

"Listen to this!" Fin gave a shout of laughter, then read aloud, "'Sources close to Catherine Lindsay report actually having seen her stroll the beach with her dead husband.' Where in hell d'you s'pose they got that?"

"Perhaps they," Cathy suggested sweetly, "have also suffered a nasty crack on the head."

Fin glowered, but otherwise refused to rise to the bait.

"I wonder," Noel said, "who these 'sources close to Catherine Lindsay' are?"

"Noel, really." Cat plucked a handkerchief from her emerald-green sleeve, dabbed it on her tongue and wiped the newsprint stains off her fingertips. "Can't you guess?"

"Honestly, no," he returned.

"Your compatriots didn't fill your head with tales of all the weird doings around here?" Cat paused to tuck the hankie back into her sleeve. "That's not why you jumped every time a floorboard creaked or the wind moaned? That's not why you went tearing out of here within a week like the rest of them?"

"I limped out of here, hardly able to walk, if you'll recall," Noel shot back, "from trying to sleep on those slabs of concrete you call beds!"

"A board under the mattress is good for the spine!"

"Not mine!"

During his brief career as a dancer, Noel had injured his back in a fall similar to Cat's backstage tumble at the Shubert. Periodically it flared up and laid him low.

"Hold on." Fin planted an index finger in the middle of the story. "You think the chaps your son hired to write your book did this? But why would they?"

"Simple." Cat sniffed. "Those who can, write—those who can't, blab to the tabloids."

"Oh, c'mon," Cathy said deprecatingly. "That's just a little too pat, don't you think?"

"What would you know about it?" Cat swung around to face her, two bright spots burning in her cheeks. "You've been here two whole days and haven't written a *single* word!"

"When have I had the chance?" Cathy retorted. "Who sent me off to meet the 'bum what lives down the beach'?"

"Is that who you are?" Noel asked Fin. "I've heard about you."

"And I've heard about you," Fin replied evenly.

"Deny *those!*" Cat shrilled, in full cry now as she flung an accusatory finger at Cathy's suitcases. "Tell me you weren't heading for the hills like the rest of them!"

"Wanna hold it down? I'm debonin' a chicken out here an' it's delicate work." The four of them started and turned toward the kitchen doorway, where Helmut stood with a bloody apron around his middle and a knife the size of a machete in his hand.

"That's better," he growled and returned to his chicken.

"I carried those in for Cathy," Noel explained. "She left them in the car."

"A likely story!" Cat snorted derisively, then demanded of Cathy, "And who sent you off to gad about town?"

"I wasn't gadding, I was—"

"She was sick," Noel finished.

"Sick?" Cat paled. "What's the matter, darling girl?"

"Grandma, I'm fine. I just—"

"No, she isn't," Noel said. "She has a concussion."

"Dear God!" Cat pulled out a chair, sat Cathy down and gathered her to her bosom. "Are you all right?"

There was a tremor in her fingertips as they smoothed Cathy's frazzled hair off her forehead. Cathy glared at Noel, then hugged her grandmother's waist. And she realized there was hardly anything left of Cat, that her arms could very nearly go around her twice.

"I'm fine," Cathy repeated, catching her grandmother's hands and holding them tightly. "It's a very mild concussion. I'll have a headache for a week or so, but other than that it's no big deal."

"It happened yesterday, didn't it?" Fin asked. "When we had to bail out of my cabin, and you hit your head on that ruddy damn lump of driftwood."

Cathy nodded at him and saw that he was frowning. Was he angry or concerned? she wondered.

"Then out it goes!" Cat declared, wheeling toward the living room. "I'll not have it in my house!"

"No!" Cathy threw herself, arms flung out, in front of her grandmother.

Cat cocked her head to one side and raised an eyebrow. Fin gave her his "how hard did you hit your head" look. Even Noel eyed her curiously.

"How can you throw it away?" Cathy quickly lowered her arms. "After I went through a cabin wreck and a concussion to fetch it home for you?"

"Very well. If it means that much to you, the tiger stays." Cat smoothed one hand over her cheek. "You look pale, darling girl. Why don't you lie down?"

"I'll take your bags up," Fin volunteered.

Cathy watched him sling the tote over his shoulder and reach for the two heavy hard-shelled cases. But Noel had moved just as quickly and had already gripped the handles.

"I got 'em this far." Grunting with effort, he hefted them off the floor. "I can manage the rest of the way."

"No need, old fellow." Fin easily wrested the grips away from him. "Wouldn't want you to crawl out of here, hardly able to walk again, now would we?"

He bounded up the steps as if the luggage weighed no more than a snowflake, leaving Noel standing red faced behind him. A totally insensitive and thoroughly macho display, Cathy thought disgustedly.

"Did you say you had some notes for me, Noel?"

"Yes. I'll get them." Shoulders hunched and eyes downcast, he brushed past Cathy and Cat into the living room.

"Off to bed with you now," her grandmother murmured in her ear. "I'll take it from here."

She'd lie down for a while, Cathy decided, since her head was thudding like *The Anvil Chorus*, but she doubted she'd sleep. In the face of this latest development, it was time to call dear old Dad in Boston and ask some point-blank questions.

On her way upstairs, she met Fin. He was scowling as he turned the corner on the landing. He saw Cathy and stopped.

"I'll bring in the rest of your luggage."

"What rest?"

"Oh, knock it off, Cath," he said tiredly. "You aren't fooling anybody. I know you were leaving and so does Cat. If it's because of me—"

Cathy snorted derisively. "Don't flatter yourself."

"—you needn't bother," Fin went on, ignoring her interjection. "I've no intention of staying. As soon as I make other arrangements I'm gone, and you can have your grandma all to yourself," he said curtly and stepped around her.

"You didn't have to embarrass Noel," Cathy said turning around to tell him so.

"What was I supposed to do?" Fin glanced back at her over his shoulder. "Watch him give himself a hernia?"

"No. But you didn't have to enjoy it."

"I didn't," he said, his scowl deepening. But there was a telltale flush on the back of his neck as he turned away from her. "I'll leave your luggage outside your door."

Watching him descend the steps, Cathy muttered, "There but for the grace of a Y chromosome go I." Then she went to the telephone in her bedroom, dialed her parents' number and groaned when her mother's cheery, taped voice answered.

"Mom, this is Cathy," she said after the beep. "Call me as soon as you—"

There was a click, then Pamela Martin spoke in a breathless rush, "Cathy, where have you been? Are you not answering the phone? Is it ringing off the wall there, too?"

"No, not yet, but we've been out. I take it you've seen the *Tattler*?"

"Unfortunately. Has Cat?"

"She bought a copy to put in her scrapbook."

"It's already in your father's scrapbook."

"Are you and I the only members of this family who don't think this is funny?"

"So far, but we've yet to hear from your Aunt Patsy."

"That's odd, as sensitive as she is to negative press."

Despite her petulant, self-indulgent nature, Cathy supposed Patricia Martin had good reason to be publicity shy after her string of celebrity marriages and front-page fisticuffs with the paparazzi. Because she couldn't act her way out of a paper sack, Cat had little use for her; Lindsay despised her because she'd built a movie career for herself and her daughter Mellody on her parents' fame and connections. But Cathy, since she, too, had grown up feeling gauche and ungifted in the midst of genius, had always sympathized with her, even though she was a pain in the butt.

"Yes, it's odd," her mother agreed, "but she's the reason I'm monitoring the phone. I've already talked to Geraldo Rivera today—I'm just not up to Patsy."

"Is this a good time to talk to Dad?"

"You can *try*, if I can blast him out of his office."

"He's still revising the third act?"

"Still. The producer's waiting, the director's waiting, the cast is waiting—"

"And Dad's playing solitaire and thinking."

"You got it," her mother replied with a sigh. "Hang on."

Cathy did, for a good two minutes before Lindsay Martin, sounding edgy and distracted, came on the line.

"All right, Cathy. What's the score up there?"

"Wily old woman, one. Outclassed and outflanked granddaughter, zero."

"Is she upset about that silly story in the *Tattler*?"

"Oh, no. She thinks it's a real hoot."

"So do I. Too bad Pop's gone. He'd really get a kick out of it."

"If you think so, I'll leave him a copy in the library."

"What? *Et tu*, Cathy?"

"Hardly, Dad, but Grandma is doing some weird things."

"Like what?" he asked warily.

"Like keeping a humidor full of Autumn Orchard, and locking up the library like a vault."

"Hold it." Cathy could almost see her father putting up a hand. "Mother has made a shrine out of the library, and I can explain the pipe smoke. I caught Mother in there once smoking one of his pipes, and I nearly fainted till she told me the smell of Pop's tobacco made her feel closer to him."

"She did the same thing to my bedroom. Enshrined it, I mean. Yesterday I smelled Autumn Orchard in the library."

"Then she's still doing it," her father said quietly. "You were barely six months old when Pop died, Cathy. You don't remember him, and you never saw him with Mother, but they were completely absorbed in each other. Sometimes I wasn't sure they knew, or even cared, that anyone else was around. Until you came along. Pop thought you were the greatest thing since sliced bread."

"Really? You never told me that before."

"Never came up before." Lindsay paused, his lips smacking faintly as he drew on a cigarette. "And you know how Mother feels about you, darling girl."

Cathy laughed. "Is that why you sent me up here to do Grandma's memoirs? Not because you fired Noel?"

"Who the hell—" Her father checked his outburst, then said, "He's there, isn't he?"

"Yep. Showed up this afternoon to bring me the notes he'd compiled. I thought it odd, to say the least, that he was so eager to help me finish a book that's guaranteed to make the nonfiction best-seller list."

"I might as well tell you, then. He wants the job back. Practically got on his knees and begged for it."

"Why did you can him, Dad? Noel's your best friend."

"It was Mother's decision, but she refused to say. His back going out again gave me a good excuse, and then Mother told me to send for you."

"Me? But why—" Cathy remembered Fin then and sighed. "Never mind. I think I know why. I also think I know how this ghost story stuff got started." She told her father about Fin's uncanny resemblance to Phineas.

"Interesting. Everyone supposedly has a double someplace," he commented thoughtfully, then asked, "what do you know about this Fin McGraw?"

"I know he's Irish. He says he's an actor, at the Rosebriar over on Nantucket, but Grandma says he's a playwright."

"Which is it?"

"Beats me."

"Mother has always collected strays, Helmut and Had are prime examples. McGraw's probably harmless, but he is in the business, and if he looks that much like Pop . . ."

The implication in her father's unfinished thought left a bad taste in Cathy's mouth. She'd certainly considered the benefits of friendship with Catherine Lindsay to Fin's career, but the possibility that he might use his resemblance to Phineas to play on Cat's sympathies hadn't occurred to her. She wished it hadn't now.

"He's genuinely fond of Grandma," Cathy replied defensively. "He took her shopping today and—" And came back loaded like a pack mule a day after his cabin and everything he owned had washed out to sea.

"I'm rather fond of her myself," Lindsay replied pointedly. "I'd come up there if I didn't have this damn play to finish. Keep your eyes open and take care of your grandmother. Get the book written, but keep in mind she's eighty-seven. Coddle her, don't overtax her and she'll come through. She's an old trooper, you know."

"Yes, I know. And I will."

"Okay, honey, talk to you later. Bye now."

"G'bye, Dad." He hung up, and as Cathy took the phone away from her ear she heard a second click on the line.

Wily old woman, indeed.

10

LYING ON HER BED with a cold cloth over her eyes, Cathy kept seeing Cat sitting alone in the ugly, dusty library puffing on one of Phineas's pipes. Though it explained why she'd smelled Autumn Orchard, it was not a comforting image. It ached with loneliness, reminded her how frail Cat had felt in her arms and finally pushed Cathy up into a sitting position.

Her head pulsed as she swung her legs over the side, flipped the cloth over the headboard and gazed troubledly at the faded posters on the walls. How many times in the past nine years, she wondered, had Cat visited her room?

She'd probably come at night on her way to bed, padding through the sitting room in her pink chenille bathrobe to sit on the four-poster with Snoopy in her arms while she thought about the granddaughter who'd gone off to England to marry the next Olivier. The granddaughter she was lucky to get flowers from at Christmas and on her birthday.

At some point in that neglectful span of years, Fin McGraw had happened along with Granddad's face to charm his way into Cat's life. When, Cathy wondered, when had he appeared...with his navy-blue eyes, his sexy-as-hell Irish accent...and his chest...? Oh, God, his chest, his back, his shoulder blades, his mouth—

Stop it! Cathy gave herself a slap on the jaw, took a shower and washed her hair, poked her nose out into the gallery and hauled the rest of her suitcases into her room. Then she dried and curled her hair, and pressed a pair of navy trousers and a double-breasted emerald-green blouse.

When she came downstairs, Noel was standing in front of the fireplace holding the tiger belly up in his hands. Either the gasp she made or the thud of her heart against her breastbone clued him he wasn't alone; he turned abruptly on one heel and saw her on the bottom step.

"How d'you feel?" He put the saber-tooth back and came toward her.

"Much better, thanks."

"You look much better." Noel stopped in front of her, loosely caught her hands and smiled. "It's a miracle you didn't fracture your skull on that hunk of driftwood."

"With my hard head, are you kidding?"

He laughed and tugged her off the step. The dining room was lighted by the setting sun, the Spode and Waterford on the table gleamed in the thick molten beam slanting through the sheer panels of the French doors but the living room lay in deep shadow.

"The shape fascinates me," Noel said as he led her toward the tiger, "but I can't figure out what it looks like."

Play dumb, Cathy cautioned herself, feeling threatened by his interest. Don't tell him any more than you have to.

"It's a tiger. A saber-tooth tiger poised to spring."

They stopped before the fireplace, Noel letting go of her hand to cross his arms and purse his lips. "Is that what it looks like to you?"

"No." Cathy backed up to the table beside the rose velvet chair and switched on the lamp. "That's what it looks like to Grandma. That's what she told me to look for when she sent me off to fetch it."

"You mentioned that earlier." Noel turned away from the fireplace, his arms still folded. "Where'd you find it?"

"On the beach."

"I know that." He laughed. "Where on the beach?"

Who cares where, Cathy thought, but told him. "In the copse of pine trees that used to grow by Fin's cabin. They washed away with his cabin."

"That's a shame." Noel's gaze lifted past the top of her head and settled on the library doorway.

"Where is the homeless wonder, by the way?"

Noel started and blinked at her. "Hmm?"

"I said, where's Fin?"

"Oh. He took Cat for her evening stroll on the beach."

A jolt of fear raced through Cathy's body, so suddenly it left her ears ringing. "You let them go?" she demanded.

Noel looked at her blankly. "Why not?"

"Why not? Damn it, Noel! Because Fin's the one they saw on the beach with Grandma, that's why!"

"Ooh." He winced. "I didn't think."

"No kidding!"

Cathy shot through the foyer, the front door and down the porch steps. Her hair whipped in her eyes but she raked it back and ran. At the end of the boardwalk she skidded to a halt and scanned the beach. The sand glittered and the Atlantic gleamed like pewter in the late-afternoon sun. The moon hung at two o'clock in the still-daylight sky, and a flock of gulls squawked above the surf just beginning to swell with the evening tide.

Holding her hair back with both hands, Cathy glanced to her left and saw their tracks before she saw Fin and Cat coming toward her around the dunes. They were about a hundred yards away, and in no particular hurry. The pink-and-white-banded umbrella Cat carried on the beach turned slowly like a kaleidoscope behind her head. Fin walked beside her, his jeans rolled up to midcalf, his sneakers tied together over one shoulder, his hands in his pockets and his eyes on the sand as he kicked it with his bare feet.

They were following the tracks they'd made leaving Cat's House, two meandering sets of footprints that hung a left into the dunes about fifty yards from the boardwalk. Cathy frowned and squinted at the break in the trail. One set of tracks struck purposefully up the dunes, but two continued down the beach.

Fin saw it then, too. He stopped suddenly, his hair fluttering in the wind, raised his eyes from the sand—and threw himself in front of Cat. He flung out his arms to shield her as half a dozen reporters and photographers rushed them from a cleft in the dunes shouting, "Miss Lindsay! Miss Lindsay!" Their screeching voices almost drowned out the cries of the gulls wheeling overhead.

Cathy wheeled, too, saw Noel hovering on the porch, cupped her hands over her mouth, sucked a breath into her diaphragm and screamed, in her best imitation of Cat, "He-e-ell-mm-uu-tt! *He-ll-lll-mmm-uu-tt!*" Then she kicked off her espadrilles, snatched them up and ran.

A guy with a minicam hit his lights and started filming. Fin aimed a soccer-style kick at him, showering the lens with sand, then spun toward the photographer who'd grabbed a fistful of his shirt and was trying to haul him away from Cat. The heel of Fin's hand shot out, caught the photographer on the bridge of his nose and crumpled him.

The reporters split in half to outflank Fin. The strobes fired in his face, blinding him. Flinging one arm over his eyes, Fin stumbled, roaring words at them Cathy didn't understand but figured were Gaelic. He tried to keep Cat herded behind him, but the pack and Cat had sensed the weakness in his defense.

"Grandma, no!" Cathy screamed, but too late.

Cat stepped away from Fin, collapsed her umbrella and assumed a fencer's stance. "En garde!" she cried, thrusting the umbrella like a rapier.

The guy with the minicam shook the sand off his lens and raised it to his shoulder. Shrieking at him, Cathy hurled her espadrilles. They hit him on the shoulder blades and spun him around. His mouth fell open and he made a hasty exit for the dunes. Pivoting she saw Helmut loping toward her, a grim expression on his face, a newspaper clapped one-handed over his head and three gulls dive-bombing him.

"Hurry!" Cathy shouted and ran toward Cat, who was stabbing valiantly at the reporters ringed around her. Ringed and closing, shouting questions, dodging and grabbing at the tip of her umbrella.

"Leave her alone!" Cathy screamed as Fin swept an arm across his eyes and started pulling people off Cat.

Both Cat and her umbrella were beginning to wilt in the horde of hungry news hounds. Fin grabbed two photographers by their shirts and dragged them back, but a petite blonde in a denim jumper beaned him with her shoulder bag and sent him reeling. A comrade in khaki pants and a green shirt tossed sand in Fin's face, grabbed the tip of the umbrella and gave it a wrench. He not only unarmed Cat, he pulled her off her feet and onto her knees.

Helmut let out an enraged bellow, flung away the newspaper and charged past Cathy. The blonde opened her mouth to scream, but the front section of the *Tattler* floated earthward and pasted itself to her face. While she tried to free herself, Cathy hurled her espadrilles again, smacking the blonde in the jaw. She sat down hard on the sand and burst into tears. One of her fellow yellow journalists grasped a handful of her jumper and dragged her away toward the dunes.

"You'll never be Diane Sawyer!" Cathy hollered, then slid to her knees before Cat. "Oh, God! Oh, Grandma—"

"Oh, get out of the way!" Knocked down but not out, Cat gave Cathy a push and rose on her knees. "*Sic 'em,* Helmut!"

Glancing over her shoulder, Cathy saw Helmut standing on the clod in the khaki pants, his size-fourteen foot planted firmly on the photographer's chest. Rolls of exposed film littered the sand, and several cameras were looped over one of Helmut's beefy arms. He ripped the back off a Nikon as Cathy watched, and tossed the film away.

"You're lookin' at a lawsuit, Godzilla!" the squirming man screeched at him.

"Get the hell outta here," Helmut growled, dumping the cameras beside him, "before I pretend you're Tokyo."

Casting a baleful eye at the gulls hovering overhead, Helmut came to stand guard over Cat. Fin pushed himself up on his elbows and spit sand out of his mouth. Cathy, too, had sand between her teeth, Cat was covered with it, but Helmut was immaculate in the white trousers and shirt he always wore.

"You all right, Cat?" Fin panted, blinking at the tears streaming down his cheeks.

"I'm fine, dear boy, there's no need for tears."

"He's got sand in his eyes, Grandma."

"Sand, hell, I've got the whole ruddy beach in my eyes!" He tried to get up, but Cathy held him down. "Relax," she said. "Let your eyes water and flush it out."

Fin cocked his head to one side. "What's that racket?"

"It's Noel," said Cathy, glancing over her shoulder at him trotting toward them with the kitchen first-aid kit bumping noisily against his thigh, a mint-green towel and a thirty-five-millimeter camera draped around his neck.

"What *fun!*" Cat exclaimed happily. "My blood hasn't pumped like this since Errol Flynn and I dueled on the poop deck in the *Lady and the Pirate!*"

"Enjoy it while you can," Cathy advised. "We're going to be sued by every sleazy tabloid in the country for this."

"I doubt it," said Noel, dropping to one knee beside her and opening the first-aid kit. "When I saw what was happening, I grabbed my camera out of my briefcase. I've got it all on film—that pack of vultures attacking Cat, that fool throwing sand . . . and boric acid?"

"Oh, thanks, old man." Fin sighed gratefully.

Cathy wiped his face with the towel and filled the eyecup from the kit. It took several washes, but finally the sand was flushed out, and Fin grinned at her with boric acid dripping off his chin. "Want to get engaged now, or wait till after supper?"

"He's fine," she told Noel dryly, and they helped him up.

"C'mon, old lady." Helmut bent down to pick up Cat.

"I'll walk, thank you." She glared and grasped her umbrella as if she meant to hit him with it. "Old I may be, but I'm not crippled. Shaken and ill used, yes, but I—"

"Zip it," Helmut growled and lifted her effortlessly.

His bearing as regal as a palace eunuch bearing a queen, he carried Cat toward the house. Her pink-and-white umbrella popped open above their heads, and an escort of gulls swooped behind them.

"Care to be my copilot?" Fin asked, blinking at Cathy through his still-tearing eyes.

"Sure." She smiled, offering him her hand.

He ignored it and looped his right arm around her shoulders, much as he'd done the day before when they'd stumbled out of the surf, which gave Cathy no choice but to wrap her left arm around his waist. He fell easily, almost intuitively, into step with her. Noel brought up the rear, stopping along the way to pick up Fin's sneakers.

Too bad the three-legged sack race wasn't an Olympic event, thought Cathy, mindful of the rub of Fin's denim-clad thigh against hers. They'd be a sure thing for a gold, she decided as she steered him off the beach, up the boardwalk and across the porch behind Helmut.

"Egad! *Stop!*" Cat screeched as he carried her into the foyer. Helmut stopped so suddenly Cathy and Fin almost bumped into him. "Damn it to hell, my umbrella! An open one in the house is such bad luck!"

Helmut heaved a sigh and muttered. So did Cathy, while Cat fumbled to collapse the shade. The catch gave, the umbrella came down and Cat said, "Lead on, MacDuff."

Helmut did, straight through the house and up the steps.

"Is it the sand in my eyes," Fin asked Cathy, "or is Helmut actually carrying Cat up the stairs?"

"He is," she murmured, awed by the sight of Helmut majestically rounding the corner on the landing.

Two things struck her: one, Fin had to be very familiar with Cat's household to know what a momentous occurrence it was to see Helmut climbing the stairs; and two, her grandmother needed looking after.

Realizing she had to take charge, she turned smartly to face the survivors.

"Noel, find Had and put him on watch with his hoe. I'll call Dad and the police to report we've had trespassers."

"Done." Noel tossed the first-aid kit on the wing chair and went out the front door.

"As for you." Cathy placed her hands on Fin's shoulders and sat him down on the couch. "More boric acid." Then she picked up the first-aid kit and put it in his lap.

He wiped a hand over his bloodshot eyes and blinked at her. "Are you taking charge, or do I still have sand in my eyes?"

"That pack of jackals attacked my grandmother! This is war!"

"Well, blow me down," he said and grinned.

"A simple salute will do," Cathy replied, feeling a blush start up her throat.

Fin gave her a jaunty one. "Aye, aye, captain!"

"Admiral," she corrected and turned toward the stairs just as Helmut came down them.

If he'd worn a ring, Cathy would've fallen on her knees and kissed it. She opened her mouth to say thank-you, but Helmut raised an index finger the size of a stick of salami.

"Stow it," he snarled and started toward the kitchen, but swung abruptly around in the doorway. "Nice shot with the shoe, Cath. I ain't crazy 'bout the punk, but the little bimbo deserved it."

"The blonde?" the punk queried incredulously. "The one who clobbered me with her purse?"

"Yes," Cathy said, glancing at Fin over her shoulder.

He'd turned sideways to look at her over the back of the couch and the quarterdeck rail. The lamp she'd left on next to the velvet wing chair backlit the grin on his face and streaked his tousled dark hair with blue highlights.

"You threw your shoe at her?"

"I did."

"And you hit her?"

"Right in the jaw."

"Well, shiver me timbers."

There was no sarcasm in Fin's voice, only admiration. It softened his grin and shivered Cathy's timbers but good, as the lamplight and something else she dared not guess at gleamed in Fin's eyes.

Fighting like a berserker to protect Cat hardly proved his innocence—not when it made as much sense to fight to defend his entrée into the upper echelon of the theatrical world. Still, Cathy could not discount that Fin's first impulse had been to shield Cat.

Suddenly Cathy wanted Fin to kiss her again as he had on the beach. "You were magnificent," she told him sincerely.

"I don't feel magnificent. I feel like hell. Not only did those leeches best me—" his grin twisted ruefully as he bent his right elbow on the back of the sofa "—one of 'em slugged me in the ribs and I've got a killer headache."

He sighed tiredly, sweeping his wind-snarled hair off his forehead, and Cathy saw the reason for his headache. An ugly purple bruise swelled on his right temple.

"I'll get the aspirin," she said and hurried away.

When she came back with two caplets, a glass of water and a clean, wet dishcloth, Fin was lying down with two throw pillows under his head. Sitting beside him facing the fireplace, Cathy gave him the aspirins. As he raised himself on one elbow to swallow them, a strip torn out of his polo shirt near the right shoulder fell open. Sand clung to the good-size patch of chest hair beneath.

Fin drank the water, handed her the glass and sighed as he lay back down on the cushions. Cathy took a fortifying sip, set the water aside and leaned over him to press the cloth gently on his temple. The movement gaped the draped front of her blouse and laid her elbow against his warm bare skin.

"Ahh," Fin said with a sigh, his eyes drifting shut, his deeply expelled breath sending a shiver across Cathy's exposed right collarbone.

"There's a really nasty bruise here," she said, doing her best to ignore the proximity of his lips to her breast.

"I saw stars."

"So did I when I hit my head on the tiger."

"How's your headache?"

"Actually, it's gone," she answered, surprised.

Fin opened his eyes to the lace edge of her camisole no more than an inch from his nose.

"God, I love this blouse," he said thickly.

"Me, too," Cathy murmured, almost as much as she loved the Irish lilt in Fin's voice, his navy-blue eyes, his gentleness with Cat, his sense of humor, the sand in his chest hair...

"Promise me, Cath." He slid his hand inside her blouse and flattened his palm in the small of her back.

"Anything," she replied, left breathless by the seductive swirl of his fingertips.

He lifted his head slightly to rub his nose along the lace edge and whispered, "Never wear it for anyone but me."

"Oh—" Cathy swallowed as Fin's teeth closed on the lace and nibbled. "I—" A shiver raced through her as the tip of his tongue touched her skin. "Oh, Fin, darling." She moaned as he traced a path to the hollow of her throat.

Tipping back her head, Cathy pressed his face to her breast. She forgot about Cat, the reporters, the police. She even forgot Fin had to breathe, so lost was she in the sensations stirred by his tongue, until he broke away from her, gasping for breath.

"Oh, darling, I'm sor—"

"Hush." Fin sucked a deep breath, took her face in his hands and drew her lips toward his.

Something moved, no flashed, near the fireplace, drawing Cathy's mesmerized gaze from the curve of his mouth to the mantel—and a wink of light jeweling in the tiger's right eye. A shriek tore past her lips and Fin let out a howl. Cathy shot to her feet and so did he, clutching his torn shirt. He drew his hand away slowly, gaped first at the angry red skids left by her nails, then at the mantel, and finally at Cathy.

"Oh, Fin!" She reached to touch the scratches, but drew back her fingers when he slapped his hand over them.

"What the hell was that for?" He winced as he rubbed his chest. "A simple 'Not tonight, we both have a headache' would've sufficed."

"Oh, no! It's not that! It's—" Cathy bit her bottom lip, thinking fast "—a mouse! I saw a mouse!"

Fin cocked a dubious eyebrow at her. "On the mantel?"

"Yes, on the mantel." Oh, how flimsy, she thought. "It ran across and ducked behind the candles."

"Well, then." Fin swept up the tiger and cocked it like a hammer. "We'll fix the little blighter."

"No!" Cathy jumped at him and clamped both hands around the tiger. "You'll break it!"

"It's only a lump of driftwood." Fin looked at her askance. "But you nearly had apoplexy when Cat threatened to throw it out. Maybe it isn't just a lump of driftwood."

"Oh, don't be silly!"

"Let's see who's being silly."

With a twist of his wrist, Fin wrenched the tiger out of her grasp and examined it under the lamp beside the wing chair. Her jaw clenched, Cathy watched him roll the saber-tooth belly up in his hands and lean closer to the light. She didn't feel threatened as she had with Noel, just angry.

"Ah, here it is—the *Rachel Simms*." He straightened and turned toward her. "D'you know what this is?"

"Yes," Cathy replied coolly.

"What, then?"

"None of your business," she snapped.

"None of my business. Well. Then I think I've got the straight of it at last." Fin put the saber-tooth back between the candlesticks and faced her. "I thought you didn't like me, but I was wrong. You like me well enough when it suits you. But you don't trust me, do you?"

"I scarcely know you."

"That didn't seem to matter on the couch," Fin replied bluntly. "Distrust is based on fear, y'know. What're you afraid of?"

"It's also based on ignorance," Cathy countered icily.

"I see." Fin crossed his arms. "I should submit my résumé, should I? And perhaps three personal references?"

"Stop it! Of course not! You know perfectly well—"

"Good. 'Cause my life is none of your business." He snatched up the tiger again and thrust it, none too gently, into her hands. "Sleep with this tonight," he said and strode past her out of the living room.

11

HER FACE FLAMING, Cathy squeezed her eyes shut and listened to Fin's footsteps pound up the stairs. When his bedroom door slammed, she winced, opened her eyes and looked at the tiger. It lay dull and lifeless in her hands.

She hated it, despised it, wanted to throw it back in the sea. Her life had been nothing but a shambles since she'd found it and . . . No. Her life had been a shambles before she'd found the tiger, before she'd met Fin McGraw. She just hadn't realized it.

Fin was right; she was afraid. Afraid of the way he made her feel, of the way she wanted to feel, of the things she wanted to say to him, do to him . . .

"Hey, Cath!"

She jumped at Helmut's voice, nearly dropping the tiger, and clutched it possessively to her breast. Very much the same way she'd clutched Fin. Her face scalding again, Cathy looked at Helmut in the kitchen doorway.

"Anybody gonna eat tonight?" he asked testily. "This chicken's gettin' pretty long in the beak."

Sighing distractedly, Cathy returned the saber-tooth to the mantel. Her nerve endings were still tingling, the lace edge of her camisole damp and clinging to her breasts. Her headache had returned.

"Would you fix a tray for Grandma? Since she hasn't come down yet, maybe I can get her to stay upstairs and rest."

"Okeydoke. You want somethin'?"

"No, thanks, I'm not hungry."

Helmut went back to the kitchen, leaving Cathy staring at the saber-tooth. "What are you?" she murmured.

The tiger didn't answer, not that it would've surprised her if it had, because it wasn't just a lump of driftwood. It was a piece of Captain Croft's ship, but it was something else, too.

Recalling the moment she'd discovered *Rachel Simms* burned into the saber-tooth's belly, Cathy felt again the certainty that it meant something. But she still couldn't get a handle on what. Tell me, she wanted to shriek at the tiger, talk to me. C'mon, damn it, you winked at me, why won't you talk?

Because it can't, Cathy reasoned, bending her elbow on the mantel and curling her knuckles against her chin, so it winks instead. It winks because it can't talk, so a wink means . . . a wink means . . .

"A wink means I have a concussion and I'm still seeing things that aren't really there," she said, leaning nose to gnarled nose with the tiger. "It also means I'm talking to a piece of driftwood."

Shaking her head, she went to the kitchen for her grandmother's tray and carried it upstairs. Cat was in bed reading, propped on a pink satin backrest, her half lenses sliding down the slope of her long nose. The bathroom door was partially closed, muffling the sound of the tub draining, and the lamp was on. The smoke from the cigarette between her fingers snaked a thin blue trail toward the light.

"Aren't you wonderful to bring me my supper!" Cat slapped the book she held shut, laid it down on its red leather cover and gave it a nudge under the pillow.

"And aren't you sensible to put yourself to bed," Cathy said approvingly as she placed the tray in her lap.

"Of course I am. You can't live as long as I have behaving like a peahen."

"Then what's this?" Cathy pinched the cigarette from her and tsked. "This is not sensible."

"This is my only remaining vice." Cat snatched it back and took a long drag.

"I meant smoking in bed, Grandma."

"At my age, a cigarette is the only fire I'm likely to have in my bed."

Cathy chuckled. "I'm going to take a shower."

She did, then cleaned up the sand that had spilled out of her clothes and Cat's, put on a pair of light blue sweats and socks and called the police. The response was less than sympathetic until she said the magic words—Catherine Lindsay—and the cop snapped to and promised more frequent patrols.

Amused, Cathy hung up. She was accustomed to Catherine Lindsay's name being tantamount to "open sesame," but she'd never understood it. Her grandmother's fame had always seemed as commonplace as the fact she had blue eyes. On the other hand, her Aunt Patsy had elevated dropping Cat's name to an art form. And Mellody was following in her footsteps.

It struck Cathy then that she had yet to see Fin drop so much as a syllable. And now that she thought about it, there was no reverence in Fin's manner toward Cat, either. Only affection.

But Patsy and Mellody gave flatterers everywhere a bad name. Having observed firsthand every obsequious nuance, Cathy realized with a slow, sinking feeling starting in the pit of her stomach, she would've spotted it in Fin, if it were there.

Why hadn't she realized this before? Probably because she hadn't thought about her aunt in years until her mother mentioned her on the phone, or about Mellody since she'd thrown away the voodoo doll. Was late really better than never, or had she already hopelessly blown things with Fin?

There was only one way to find out and that was to face him. But never do tonight what you can put off until tomorrow. Morning would be soon enough, she decided, picking up the phone and dialing her parent's number. Again, her mother broke in to the recorded message as soon as she heard Cathy's voice.

"Make my day, Mom. Tell me Dad is typing the last line of act three even as we speak."

"Uh-oh. What happened?"

Cathy told her and assured her Cat wasn't hurt.

"I'm glad to hear that. As for your father, all I can tell you is he's locked himself in his study."

"Well, it's a beginning."

"It'd better be near the end. Next time he wanders out to go to the bathroom, I'll tell him what's happened."

"Have you heard from Aunt Patsy?"

"Not yet. Why do you ask?"

"Just curious." She said good-night to her mother, opened her suitcases and started unpacking. She'd nearly finished when Cat appeared in the sitting room doorway with the tray.

"Would you take this to the kitchen for me, darling?"

"Sure. Would you care for anything else?"

"Thank you, no. I'm fine."

Like hell, thought Cathy, noting the shuffle in her steps, a sure sign of stiffness, as Cat carried the tray to the dresser. "Anything hurt, Grandma?"

"My pride," Cat replied ruefully. "Ten years ago, I'd've made shish kebab out of them all."

"I think your doctor should examine you."

"For what? Sore knees and aches and pains?"

"At your age, sore knees should be seen by a doctor."

Cat glared at her imperiously. "I am the grandmother, you are the grandchild. Don't hover."

"I'm not hovering. I'm coddling."

"I despise coddlers. A good night's sleep and I'll be ready to write my memoirs first thing in the morning."

"All right, then, tell you what. I'll unpack my computer this evening and we'll hit the book bright and early in the morning. Say, nine o'clock in the library?"

The library!

None of the shock in her voice showed in Cat's face. She merely looked puzzled—but then, so was Cathy. She hadn't planned to suggest the library as a place to work, it just popped out when she opened her mouth.

"On second thought, why not?" Cat tapped a finger on her chin. "A quiet place to write has always been its function."

"But if you'd rather not, I mean, if you object—"

"Why on earth would *I* object?" The emphasis Cat gave the pronoun suggested, however, that someone else might. "I think it's an excellent suggestion. And high damn time, too. Now if you'll excuse me, darling, I'm very tired."

"But Gran—"

The sitting room door closed in Cathy's face. What on earth had possessed her to suggest the library? Cathy picked up the tray and headed for the kitchen.

There were no lights on in Fin's bedroom, only the single lamp in the living room and the recessed floods in the kitchen. Even Helmut's room was empty, though the brass floor lamp next to his morris chair was lit. A book lay open on the cushioned seat, as if he'd risen quickly, put the book aside and gone.

"This is weird," Cathy murmured, standing in the doorway and wondering where everyone had gone to.

Then, because she couldn't resist the temptation, she stepped into Helmut's room. Like the man, it was immaculate. The glass cabinets built into the walls above the wainscoting originally to hold dishes now contained books, mostly, she saw, the works of Conan Doyle bound in leather, and an exquisite collection of scrimshaw.

She didn't touch anything, just looked around to satisfy her curiosity, then returned to the kitchen and filled a mug with water to make herself a cup of cocoa in the microwave. As she shut off the tap, her gaze lifted to the window above the sink, and the shadowy figure darting across the expanse of lawn between the guest cottage and the greenhouse.

"Damn those reporters!" Dumping her mug in the sink, Cathy beat a hasty path to the Dutch door. One of them had gotten past Had and his hoe, but they'd get no farther, she vowed as she slipped outside into the chilly spring night.

Her stocking feet made no noise on the flagstone patio or the steps leading to the lawn. Letting her eyes adjust to the darkness, Cathy crept down the steps, inhaling the musty smell of dew-soaked earth and the tang of the ocean. She reached the last stair, paused to listen for the whisper of footsteps above the murmur of the surf, then moved to step onto the lawn—and spilled face first in the grass.

A trip wire, Cathy realized as she pushed herself up on one hand and swept her hair out of her face with the other. Someone had stretched a trip wire across—

"Gotcha!" Fin closed one hand like a clamp between her shoulder blades, gathered a fistful of sweatshirt, hauled her to her feet and flung her around. "Cath! What the hell are you doing out here? Cat was s'posed to—I mean, I thought you were—"

"I could've broken my neck!" Cathy jerked free of him and pulled down her rumpled shirt. "What the hell are you doing out here stringing trip wires?"

"I asked you first," Fin retorted, crossing his arms over the dark pullover he wore. Cathy couldn't see much of his face, only the outline of his nose and jaw and the flutter of his hair in a skitter of breeze from the beach.

"Fine. Let's be childish," she snapped. "I saw somebody skulking around the greenhouse. I figured it was one of the reporters and—"

"The greenhouse, eh? C'mon, then." He grabbed her hand and pulled her into a run behind him.

"Hold it!" Cathy dug her stocking heels into the wet grass, slipped, but nonetheless managed to turn Fin around. "What're we doing?"

"Trying to catch the bugger," he said and jerked her forward again.

"But shouldn't we—"

"Shh!" Fin slowed their pace and flattened his shoulder blades against the west wall of the greenhouse.

Cathy pressed her back to the glass beside him and lowered her voice to a whisper. "Wouldn't it make more sense to—"

"Will you shut up?" Fin rolled on his left shoulder and caught Cathy's chin in his right hand.

"In a minute. After I—"

"Now, damn it. Before you give us away."

"I think we should—"

Fin brought his mouth down over hers. Cathy's lips, parted to finish the sentence, gave his tongue instant and erotic access. His fingers slipped from her chin, threaded their way through her hair and curved around the nape of her neck. Silenced and shaken by the intensity of the kiss, Cathy swayed against him. Fin broke away from her then, taking a deep, unsteady breath.

"Now—will you shut up?"

"On one condition."

"What's that?"

"Promise to kiss me like that once a day."

"Done." He touched a fingertip to her lips, then caught her hand and drew her slowly down the length of the greenhouse.

When they reached the corner, Fin peered around it, his eyes darting left and right. Then he leaned back beside Cathy and turned his head to look at her.

"Don't see a thing," he whispered, "but we'll wait a minute and make sure."

She nodded, a delicious shiver prickling up her neck as he began to rub slow, seductive circles on her knuckles with his thumb. In the moonlight glinting off the glass panels behind them, she could see the half smile on his face, the fullness of his lower lip.

"Didn't hurt yourself when you fell, did you?"

"No," Cathy whispered.

"Good," Fin murmured, sliding his shoulder closer to hers. "I behaved like an ass earlier and I'm sorry. It's no excuse, but I've got a temper to match the accent."

"Me, too." Cathy laid her cheek lightly against his warm shoulder. "And I'm not Irish."

Fin raised his hand to touch her face, then stiffened at the rustle of slow, furtive footsteps beyond the greenhouse. Pressed against his back, Cathy leaned with him around the corner. With a startled yelp, she stumbled and fell forward on her knees as a giant white hand snaked suddenly out of the darkness, closed on the front of Fin's pullover and jerked him off his feet. Catching herself on her hands, Cathy looked up and saw Fin, dangling a good six inches off the ground from Helmut's huge left fist. She also saw Had, his hoe cocked menacingly over one shoulder.

"It's me," Fin said dryly.

With a snarl, Helmut dropped him. He fell with a thump on his tailbone and the heels of his hands next to Cathy.

"Thought you was him," Had said, lowering his hoe.

"Same here," Fin replied, levering himself to his feet with one hand and pulling Cathy up with the other. "Nice job, lads. We've managed to catch one another. Where's Penney?"

"Figured he was with you," Helmut said.

"Well, he's not. When'd you see him last?"

"Dunno," Had said.

Helmut shrugged.

"Now listen," Fin replied testily, "and this time let's get it right. I've got the back of the house, you two've got the front."

"Coulda sworn you said we had the back," Had said.

"No, I said you have the front."

"Yep." Had nodded. "That's what y'said, all right. You got the front, we got the back."

Helmut folded his arms and scowled. Fin sighed and pinched the bridge of his nose.

"You'd better go keep an eye on Cat," he said to Cathy, brushing his thumb lightly across her knuckles before releasing her hand. "This may take a while."

With her fingers no longer threaded warmly through Fin's, Cathy felt the nip in the night air and the dew soaking through her socks. She nodded and went, reluctantly, pausing at the foot of the steps to look back at the three of them still wrangling by the corner of the greenhouse.

Sighing distractedly, she took a giant step over the trip wire, hurried up the stairs, across the patio and into the kitchen. Noel was there in a navy sweater and slacks, red nosed and sniffling, leaning against the drainboard, gulping instant coffee from the mug she'd left in the sink.

"Caught me," he said guiltily. "But damn, it's cold out there."

"Don't worry, I'm not a stoolie," Cathy told him with a smile. "But the Keystone Cops are looking for you."

"Double oops." He made a face, put down the mug and made for the door.

"Watch out for the trip wire at the bottom of the steps."

He waved and went outside, closing the door behind him. Slowly, her mind on Fin and their kiss, Cathy picked up the mug and took it to the sink to rinse it. Had and Helmut and Fin had disappeared from the corner of the greenhouse, and she didn't see Noel, either. She must have missed him crossing the lawn, she thought, shutting off the water and turning the mug upside down on the drainboard.

But she didn't miss the two solid thumps that came suddenly from overhead. Grandma! Cathy thought, whirling out of the kitchen and racing up the steps. On the landing she saw Cat's door was closed, but the door to the attic, which lay between her bedroom and Cat's, stood open. Light spilled down the narrow flight of steps.

Cathy flew along the gallery and took the attic stairs two at a time. Her stocking feet slipped on the uncarpeted steps, sending her up them headfirst and falling. She managed to grab the banister, twist herself around and sit down hard with a spine-jarring whump on the top stair.

"What an entrance!" Cat applauded vigorously.

"Grandma! I thought you were in bed!" Cathy gaped at her grandmother, who was bent on her knees about six feet away beside two overturned cardboard boxes in front of a wall full of shelves.

"Obviously not," she replied as she righted one of the boxes. "I thought some of my older scrapbooks might jog my memory, so I came up to get them. Unfortunately I knocked this stuff down in the process."

"I'll put it back." Cathy got to her feet and helped her grandmother off the floor. Cat winced a little and her knees cracked like dry twigs as she stood.

"Thank you, darling girl." She gave her cheeks an affectionate squeeze, picked up the green leather albums and made for the stairs.

Two boxes, two thumps, Cathy thought as she lifted the cartons back onto the shelves. Obviously that's what she'd heard, but as long as she was up here, she might as well have a look. Just to make sure.

The servants' quarters in Captain Croft's day, the attic was a series of five rooms: a large main chamber and four smaller ones off a narrow hall. The first held Cat's wardrobe trunks, another mostly furniture, the third a mishmash. The fourth room, the farthest and smallest on the left, held Captain Croft's sea chests and nothing else. Not even dust. Cathy stopped. The floor was gray with dust, so was the octagon window tucked beneath the eaves, but the weathered wooden chests were slick as a whistle.

"Uh-oh," Cathy muttered, stooping her way across the slope-ceilinged room.

Dropping to her knees, she wiped her middle finger across the lid of a four-by-six footlocker with a warped bottom and rubbed it against her thumb. No dust. Then she raised the lid. The maps and charts inside had been undone from their carefully rolled tubes and pawed through in obvious haste, the fragile old parchment torn in places and badly creased. She quickly discovered the other chests were in the same shape.

The spotless lids made sense: no dust, no fingerprints. Shaking with fury, Cathy rocked back on her heels. Who the hell had done this and why? What had they been looking for among Captain Croft's sea charts and cargo manifests?

Then she remembered Fin holding the tiger in his hands, reading *Rachel Simms* without a flicker of surprise in his voice. He'd known what the saber-tooth was; the missing *i* hadn't tripped him at all. But, she argued with herself, it was hardly an indictment, since Cat's House was built around bits and pieces of the ship, and anyone who spent any time here would know it.

Now that was an interesting thought. There'd been eight other people in residence of late. Tomorrow she'd put the chests to rights, Cathy decided, and took herself downstairs to her grandmother's room.

Cat was back in bed, her glasses on, one of the scrapbooks open on her knees.

"Someone's been in Captain Croft's chests," Cathy told her as she sat down beside her, "and left them in a frightful mess."

"Really? How odd." Cat turned a page brittle with dried glue. "You're the only person who's ever shown the slightest interest in his things."

"Whoever did it wiped all the dust off so they wouldn't leave fingerprints."

"Oh, really!" Cat laughed, lowering her chin to look over her glasses. "More than likely they wiped off the dust so they wouldn't get their hands filthy."

"That's possible," Cathy granted grudgingly, "but I can't imagine who'd give a rip one way or the other about the captain's sea charts. Can you?"

"No. But I can't imagine why you do, either." Cat laid the scrapbook aside and her glasses on top of it. "Perhaps Captain Croft rifled the chests himself! Perhaps he is the ghost!"

"There's no such thing as ghosts," Cathy snapped.

"Of course there isn't. Not in the Dickensian sense, at any rate. There are spiritual guides and teachers, souls who are drawn to us—"

"Grandma, please." Cathy groaned imploringly, pressing the heel of one hand to the bridge of her nose. "Don't drag me out on the limb with you and Shirley. Not tonight, not after the day I've had."

"You look pale again. Has your headache come back?"

"With a vengeance," Cathy said irritably, for it had, thudding inside her skull like blows from a sledgehammer. Maybe she had hurt herself falling over the trip wire.

"Come to Grandmama." Cat held out her arms, drew Cathy close and began gently rubbing her temples.

Her soft, cool touch felt so good, gradually relaxing Cathy and taking the edge off the wicked pounding. The fatigue beneath it, the bone-deep weariness, made her yawn and her eyes drift shut.

"Rest now," Cat murmured, massaging smooth, hypnotic circles across her brow. "Rest, and remember . . . there are more things in heaven and earth than are dreamt of in your philosophy."

"Sure thing," Cathy mumbled, rolling sleepily onto her side. "G'night, sweet prince."

"Good night, my darling Horatio."

12

WHEN SHE WOKE UP in Cat's bed the next morning, Cathy not only couldn't remember falling asleep, she couldn't remember leaving Boston three days ago, London a day before that or, for a horrifying five seconds, leaving Garrett. She shot bolt upright, heart pounding, just as her sluggish, overstressed brain kicked into wake-up-and-smell-Grandma's-stale-cigarette-butts-in-the-ashtray mode. Time fell back into place then, and the shriek welling up in her throat came out as a moan of relief.

"Still the headache?" Cat asked, turning around at her dressing table.

"No." Cathy sighed again and swept her hair out of her eyes. "Just for a second there I thought I was Pam Ewing."

Cat laughed and put down her tortoiseshell brush. "'We are such stuff as dreams are made on,'" she quoted blithely, then sprang to her feet and swept up a pair of gloves.

Ugly gloves. Really ugly—electric-yellow, stitched out of canvas. Gardening gloves.

"Grandma," Cathy intoned suspiciously, "are those putter pants you're wearing?"

"Aren't they cute?" Cat plucked the baggy striped denim coveralls away from her bony hips. "Fin bought them for me yesterday. They'll be so comfortable bending over flats in the greenhouse."

"Fin bought them?" Cathy felt that sinking feeling in her stomach again. "But—" she wanted to ask, "With what?" but changed it to "—why?"

"They struck his fancy." Her grandmother gave Cathy a catbird smile. "And because he's very fond of me."

"Has he bought you anything else?"

"Several things. Why do you ask?"

"Just nosy." Cathy smiled and glanced at the bedside clock. "It's ten past nine, Grandma. We're supposed to be bending over my computer writing your memoirs."

"We can't until you unpack the thing," Cat replied logically. "And you're such a grouch until you have your coffee—I refuse to bend over anything with you until you've had at least three cups. By then, Hadley and I will have the tomato flats all seeded."

"Uh-huh." Cathy smirked. "Quicker than you can say Jack Robinson, I suppose."

"Why, of course." Cat smiled brightly, squeezed Cathy's cheeks together in one ugly gloved hand and smacked a kiss on her mouth. "Did you ever wonder, darling girl, who the hell Jack Robinson was?"

"There are several theories, actually. One, that he was a character in a play, another—"

"Oh, you *would* know." Cat rolled her eyes and made for the door. There she paused and looked back over her shoulder. "'Misery acquaints a man with strange bedfellows,'" she said and swept out of the room.

The grouch would've laughed, but she was in the throes of a yawn so huge it threatened to unhinge her jaw. Jet lag, Cathy thought sourly, what's next? Saint Vitus' dance? Beriberi? Split ends? No—toothpaste, she decided. Her mouth tasted like something that had been too long in aluminum foil in the back of the fridge.

After she'd flossed, brushed her hair as well as her teeth, showered and dressed, Cathy felt nearly human. Her irritation at Cat flitting off to the greenhouse had faded, but she still felt uneasy. For no good reason she could think of beyond the unholy scare she'd had waking up.

Maybe she'd been having a nightmare; maybe that's why she'd warped out for a second and why she couldn't shake off the feeling, not even as she recalled Cat's apropos quote from the *Tempest* and chuckled. Then she remembered the way Fin had kissed her last night, and the chuckle in her throat changed to a whimper. She'd fallen asleep in the wrong bed, that's what it was. Lust, pure and simple. Which definitely wasn't pure, and certainly not simple.

But there it was, the overwhelming desire she'd felt since yesterday's melee on the beach to have Fin kiss her again. And now that he had it was even stronger, so strong that Cathy's fingertips trembled as she raised them to her lips. Was this what Cat had wanted her to discover when she'd told her to go look in Fin's eyes?

"So okay, I've found it," Cathy murmured troubledly. "Now what do I do with it?"

With a distracted sigh, she went to her room, put her boxed computer monitor on top of the crated disk drive, picked them up and headed for the stairs. First she'd have her coffee, then vacuum the library, hook up the PC . . .

A yard or so shy of the closed guest bathroom door, Cathy paused and leaned the stacked boxes on the gallery rail. What the heck had she done with the cables? Were they in her tote or one of her suitcases? She remembered packing them, but decided to get this stuff downstairs before instigating a search.

Taking a firmer grip on the boxes, Cathy eased them off the rail and started toward the stairs. When she reached the guest bathroom door, it swung inward and Fin stepped through it in a cloud of steam with a yellow towel knotted low and loose around his waist. So low and so loose that

Cathy's mouth went dry at the sheen of taut, wet muscle, the slash of his hipbones and the droplets of water jeweling in his dark chest hair.

Her fingers went slack, too, and if Fin hadn't made a quick grab, the disk drive listing slowly out of her grasp would've hit the floor along with Cathy's jaw. The upward lift of his left hand under the right corner helped her recover her grip, but her aplomb, the three-thousand-dollar PC and the knotted towel clenched in Fin's right hand were taking a rapid nosedive toward the blue runner underfoot.

"Which one do I drop?" he asked her quickly. "The towel or the computer?"

"The towel."

"I was hoping you'd say that." Fin let go and slid his hand beneath the left corner of the disk drive. The towel fell with a damp plop around his ankles. Smiling at her over the boxed monitor with just the right side of his mouth, he suggested softly, "What d'you say we put this down now and retire to my room?"

"I was hoping you'd say that," Cathy said with a fervent sigh.

"On three, then. One, two—"

But on three, Noel's bedroom door opened on the opposite side of the gallery. He saw Cathy and Fin as he came through it and hastily put down his briefcase. "Hang on!" he said, cutting quickly toward them across the landing.

Cathy wanted to cry; Fin muttered something under his breath and frowned at Noel as he came up beside them.

"I'm not even going to ask how you managed to end up like this," Noel said, fighting a losing battle with a grin. "Just tell me what you want me to do."

"Go away," Fin told him bluntly.

Noel laughed; apparently, he thought Fin was kidding. "Want me to take your end?"

"No, just pick up my towel." Fin sighed irritably and glanced longingly at Cathy. "Where do you want these?"

"The library, please."

Noel retrieved the towel. Fin started backward down the stairs, and Cathy followed, stealing a breath-catching glimpse of his hairy, well-muscled left leg as they turned the corner on the landing.

With Noel hovering alongside, they made it down the steps, across the dining room and living room. Noel put his briefcase beside the rose wing chair and went ahead of them into the library to move Phineas's humidor and pipe rack. Fin went in front of the desk, Cathy behind it. They put the PC down in the middle and smiled at each other.

"D'you have any plans for the next hour or so?" Noel asked Fin.

"Nothing urgent," he lied, taking the towel from him and shooting Cathy a smoldering sideways glance as he tied it in a knot over his left hip.

"In that case, I could use a lift to the ferry."

"I guess what I have to do can wait." He looked at Cathy again, this time questioningly.

She bit her bottom lip and nodded.

"Then I'll get dressed." Fin strode briskly out of the library, the bottom edge of the towel playing a seductive game of peekaboo with his right thigh.

"I'd kill for legs like that," Noel said, shaking his head as he walked out of the library.

"So would I." Cathy sighed, sagging weakly against the door frame behind him. "I wish you'd stay."

"No can do. I've got a dinner date with my agent and my editor in New York." Noel collected his briefcase from beside the chair, came back and curved one hand around her cheek. "Pluck up, honey. He'll be back before you know he's gone."

"Huh?" Cathy blinked innocently.

"Huh, hell." Noel grinned and planted a light kiss between her eyes. "Keep me posted."

"I don't suppose you could reschedule your dinner date, could you? Just for a couple of days, I mean, till things calm down around here and Daddy finishes his play and—"

"Would you stop feeling unsure of yourself?" Noel smiled and raised an eyebrow. He had such eloquent eyebrows. "You are a very capable person, Cathy."

"Then why do I have this overwhelming urge to cling to your knees and beg you not to leave me like this?"

"That's not a bad thought," he told her gently, "but I'm the wrong man."

The right man, if Cat could be trusted, came bounding down the stairs then in jeans, a blue plaid shirt and untied sneakers with no socks.

"Ready?" Fin asked, twirling his car keys around his index finger. He'd run a comb through his wet hair, and his shirt was only half-buttoned.

"As I'll ever be," Noel replied and went ahead of him out the veranda doors. Behind him, Fin paused to look back at Cathy. "I'll be back soon," he said with a simmering smile and left.

"Hurry," Cathy whispered, then went in search of coffee and the vacuum cleaner.

She made do with a quick vacuum and a spritz or two of polish on her grandfather's desk. There was plenty of room for her computer and Phineas's humidor and pipe rack, which Noel had moved to the far corner next to the lamp.

Then she uncrated the PC, plugged it in and fed it its disks, and decided that rather than search for the cables, which she didn't need until she connected the printer, she'd take a shot at a first draft of chapter one. She'd begin the story in Aunt Elvira's parlor, she thought, and sat down in her grandfather's high-backed red leather chair. Her fingers poised on the keys, Cathy waited for inspiration to strike. It didn't, so she plowed into her grandmother's life story without it and ended up floundering after six and a half abysmal pages.

Her similes were trite, and her metaphors were mixed when they weren't just plain awful. It was the most maddening stint at the computer she'd ever spent, because she could feel the right words in her head, but when she closed her eyes to concentrate on them, all she saw was Fin's wet, naked chest.

She hit the store button, recalled the file, read it and cringed. This was not the work of a well-educated and very capable person. This was the work of a sex-starved divorcée with no more imagination than a navy bean. And a brain of about the same size. Time to play solitaire and think.

But not about her grandfather's white meerschaum, which was the first thing to snag Cathy's attention as she got up from the computer. The second was the memory of Fin's right thigh peeking through the towel; the third, the solid thud she heard against the side of the house.

Cathy went to the window and looked outside at Had, wearing a carpenter's apron and jockeying a wooden ladder into place beside the shutters blown loose in the storm. He raised one foot on the bottom rung to test the stability; the ladder wobbled precariously, and Cathy held her breath until he stepped down. Then she ran outside.

"Morning, Had," she said, slowing down as she rounded the house. "Are you and Grandma finished with the tomatoes?"

"Yep. Miz Linzay's repottin' hydrangeas."

He made an adjustment to the ladder, tried the bottom rung again, but it slid to the left. Cathy caught it and steadied it against the house.

"She didn't ask you to fix the shutters, did she?"

"Nope. That actor feller said he'd nail 'em up, but that was two day ago, an' there's gonna be another blow by t'morrow night fer sure."

"Then let me do it. I can drive a straight nail."

"Glad to." He took off the apron, handed it to her and meandered away toward the garden.

Cathy's carpentry experience was limited to building a birdhouse out of ice cream sticks in Girl Scouts, but the job didn't look that difficult. She could see the empty holes in the hinged brackets securing the shutters to the window frames. There were two pouches full of shiny new nails in the apron and a clawhammer dangling from a loop.

The tricky part was getting the ladder firmly planted. She managed it at last, by borrowing two fieldstones from the border edging the flower bed beneath the windows, tied on her apron and climbed. She made her way up gingerly at first, but the ladder was as steady as the rocks she'd wedged behind the legs.

The first shutter she tackled was merely loose; Cathy had it back on its hinges and solidly nailed into place in minutes. With a feeling of accomplishment she leaned back on the ladder and admired the squarely hung shutter. It felt good to whack the living hell out of something. What unease? What sexual frustration? What—

"—the bloody hell are you doing up there?"

Startled, Cathy dropped the hammer, grabbed a rung and looked over her right shoulder at Fin. He stood behind her, gripping the ladder in both hands, his left foot braced on the bottom rung.

"I'm doing your work," she told him coolly.

"You're doing your best to break your damn neck, you mean," he said, looking as if he'd rather do it himself.

"Says you!"

"Says anybody daft enough to climb a ladder held in place by ruddy rocks!"

"The ruddy rocks work just fine!"

"Do they now?"

He stepped back, the ladder quivered and listed to the left. Yelping, Cathy flung her arms around it and clung for dear life, but Fin put his foot on the rung again and leaned back, using his body as a lever to steady the ladder.

"Now come down from there."

Because she had no choice, Cathy did, carefully easing herself earthward. When she touched ground within the circle of Fin's arms, he caught her elbow, flung her around and pinned her against the wooden rungs with his body.

"I ought to strangle you." His voice shook as he slid his hands around her throat and kissed her. A quick, hard kiss that left the imprint of his lips branded against hers.

Cathy thought he was furious, until he drew away and raised a trembling hand to her face. She realized then that she'd scared him.

"I'm sorry," Fin said. "I didn't mean to do that."

"Don't apologize. I thought you were going to choke me."

"I might yet," he threatened, curving his hand around her face. "I vacillate between wanting to throttle you and make love to you. It's very annoying."

"I can see how it would be," Cathy agreed breathlessly as his thumb softly traced her cheekbone. "If you have to pick one, I vote for the latter."

A slow smile tugged the right side of Fin's mouth. "Might be interesting. I've never done it on a ladder."

Cathy laughed giddily, until he leaned closer and traced the curve of her left eyebrow with his nose. Her breath caught and she closed her eyes, savoring the light, barely there graze.

"Come with me this afternoon," he murmured against her temple, his lips stirring a shiver across the nape of neck.

"Where to?"

"Nantucket," he said, nuzzling her ear, "to the Rosebriar so I can show you off."

Involuntarily Cathy stiffened. Only for a moment, but long enough for Fin to sense it and withdraw his hand from the curve of her throat. Oh, damn, she moaned silently. If only Noel hadn't interrupted us, if only Fin hadn't taken him to the ferry. If only he'd said come with me to the Kasbah, the moon, never-never land, anywhere but the Rosebriar Theater.

"So we're back to that, are we?"

He meant square one, not the future, but Cathy could see that dwindling rapidly away along with the warmth in his eyes. Playing dumb was her only chance. "Back to what?"

"C'mon, Cath, I'm besotted, not stupid."

"I don't know what you mean."

"The hell you don't. You can't forget who you are for five lousy minutes, can you?"

"Really," Cathy insisted, genuinely perplexed. "You've lost me."

"I never had you, and it looks like I never will. And that's too bad, 'cause Cathy Martin and I would have been damn good together." Fin touched his fingertips to her chin, then backed away from her. "But I don't care a rap for Catherine Lindsay Martin, granddaughter of the illustrious Cat Lindsay."

There was no sarcasm, just icy contempt in his voice.

"You arrogant bastard!"

"Why do you think being Cat's granddaughter is all you have to offer a man? Is it because that's all you were to that flaming egomaniac you married?"

It was a low but accurate blow, so accurate that all Cathy could do was stare at him, dazed and stricken. Had she given it away somehow, or was Fin just that perceptive?

"Real charmer, your ex." He folded his arms and smiled at her. "Classmates he and I were at the Royal Academy."

"I—I didn't know that," she stammered.

"'Course you didn't. You don't know a bloody thing about me, but you judged me nonetheless. Judged yourself, too, and we both came up wanting."

"You have no right to say that to me!"

"I've as much right to think you're a spoiled, insecure little rich brat as you have to think I'm a gigolo."

Cathy slapped him then, so hard she snapped his head around. He didn't look surprised, not even angry, just raised a hand to his jaw as he worked it back and forth.

"Now let me tell you a thing or two," she said furiously. "Cat told me you're a playwright, but you say you're an actor. You drive a brand-new Jeep, yet you lived in a hovel, and since it blew away you've been living on my illustrious grandmother's good graces! And you've got a lot of nerve calling Garrett a flaming egomaniac, 'cause you aren't much better! Your nose is so far out of joint because

I didn't swoon with desire the instant I laid eyes on you, I'm surprised you aren't breathing out of your ear!"

"Oh, really?"

"Yes, really!"

"In that case, I have one more thing to say. I read the first draft of chapter one on the monitor and it stinks."

"Oh, really?"

"Yes, really!"

"Fine, Mr. Hotshot Playwright. You write it."

"I just might."

"Be my guest."

"Not much longer, I won't." Fin picked up the ladder, moved it to the next shutter and slammed it down so hard its feet sank a good quarter inch into the ground. "There. If you break your silly neck now, it'll be your fault."

He turned and strode away toward the front of the house. So enraged she couldn't think, let alone speak, Cathy snatched the hammer out of the freshly tilled flower bed, drew back her arm and let it slip out of her fingers as Fin disappeared around the porch. It hit the ground with a thud, and a second later the screen door slammed with a resounding whap.

Cathy's quaking knees gave out on her, and she sat down hard on her tailbone next to the hammer. She'd never in her life been so mad she couldn't stand, so furious she couldn't even cry. A handful of gulls wheeled overhead, jeering at her as they veered toward the beach.

She really needed to whack the living hell out of something now. Jerking herself and the hammer off the ground, Cathy stalked up the ladder to the middle bank of shutters. At the top, she dug a nail out of her pouch, stuck it in an empty hole in one hinge, drew back the hammer and froze, her scalp tingling.

Her grandfather's red leather desk chair was turned away from the window, a curl of smoke wafting over its tall winged back.

13

SCRAMBLING DOWN THE LADDER, Cathy raced for the front door with the hammer clamped in her right hand. Up the steps and across the porch she bounded, skidding to a halt on the braided rug before the library doorway.

Her grandfather's desk chair was empty. But a thin blue ribbon of Autumn Orchard curled from the bowl of the white meerschaum in the pipe rack.

"Fin!" Cathy bellowed. "Fin!"

She bolted through the house, ricocheted off the kitchen cabinets into the back hallway and flung open the Dutch door. Had was in the rose garden, but the patio and the gazebo were deserted.

Brandishing the hammer, Cathy whirled around. Helmut, sitting with his legs crossed in his morris chair, looked up at her from the *New Yorker* without batting an eyelash.

"You lookin' for the punk?"

"Have you seen him?"

Helmut raised his thumb. "Upstairs."

"Thanks." She started away, but doubled back. "Was he in the library?"

Helmut blinked. "Nobody's ever in the library."

"Somebody was—smoking a pipe."

Helmut laughed, a basso profundo rumble deep in his chest. "Go on."

She did, taking the stairs two at a time and bursting into Fin's bedroom. It was empty. There was nothing under the bed, and nothing in the closet but his clothes. Leaving a trail of nails behind her, Cathy checked the rest of the bedrooms, hers included, the sitting room and bath and Cat's room. It, too, was empty, and there was nothing under the bed but her grandmother's slippers.

"Damn it!" She flung the fistful of bedspread she'd lifted with such force she cracked her knuckles on the bed frame, dislodging the book tucked between the mattress and the iron rail.

"Ouch!" Shaking her stinging hand, she rocked back on her heels as the red leather book Cat had been reading the night before, the one she'd tucked under her pillow when Cathy came into the room, bounced on its spine and fell open in front of her on the bedside rug.

There were two sentences underlined by a thin red ballpoint pen in the middle of the right-hand page: "A soul abruptly parted from the body—usually by means of sudden or violent death—tends to reincarnate almost immediately. Such souls tend to seek out a body of like appearance, temperament and capability to fulfill their karmic purpose."

Never die in Ireland, Cat had said during the picnic on the living room floor. But Phineas Martin had, suddenly of a burst appendix, twenty-seven years ago, and Fin McGraw had been born there—when? How old was he?

"Oh, my God—" Cathy gasped, a rush of gooseflesh racing through her body.

This was the book, the one she hadn't been able to recall, the one that had set the bells ringing in her head. She remembered the title now, too: *We Have Been Here Before*. Boy, ain't that the truth. Hastily she picked the book up, slapped it shut and stuck it back where she'd found it. She and Cat were going to have a very long talk, just as soon as she found Fin, asked him how old he was and killed him.

She made a quick reconnaissance of the attic, then took the hammer outside to search the grounds. No luck. Fin's Jeep was in the driveway, but he wasn't in it, nor was he in the garage or the guest cottage. In the greenhouse Cat was singing, "There's No Business Like Show Business" à la Ethel Merman, her voice booming through the open door. Had was spreading fertilizer around "Catherine Lindsay" and working it into the soil with a child's toy rake. Cathy trotted up to the fence.

"Have you seen Fin?"

Had stuck the plastic scoop in his hand deep in the fertilizer sack and straightened. "Nope."

"Rats." Cathy tapped the hammer distractedly against her palm. Had watched her, his sparse eyebrows drawing together over his nose. "I want to ask him a question."

"'Magin' so." Had tied the sack shut with a piece of rope. "Mebbe 'e's gone home. 'Bout time if y'ask me."

"He has no home. It blew away in the storm."

"The hell y'say." Had took out his pipe and clamped it between his teeth. "Drove by the place yesterday."

"Had," Cathy said patiently, still drumming the hammer against her hand, "I was in the shack when it blew away."

"Y'mean 'is writin' studio. Yep. It's gone fer sure. But the house warn't touched."

"What house?"

"That there steepled thing back o' the shack. Don' care much fer it m'self. Too modern."

"I see," Cathy hissed, for suddenly she did.

She saw herself staggering beside Fin up the beach, remembered tripping over the step, peering through the gloom and sheeting rain at the long-decked A-frame. The one with the security system that nobody lived in. Oh, she saw all right; she saw that she'd been had.

"That rotten, stinking—ouch!" Cathy dropped the hammer and shook her stinging hand; the more she'd thought, the harder she'd hit. Ah, but practice made perfect. She picked up the hammer and slid it firmly in the loop on her apron like a gunslinger holstering her six iron.

"E's not s'bad once y'get used t'im." Had swung the sack over his shoulder and opened the gate. "A mite lazy, but other'n that 'e's harmless."

"Practical joker, though, isn't he?"

Had shut the gate, put down the fertilizer and switched his pipe to the other side of his mouth. "Mite playful."

"And Helmut says there's never anybody in the library," Cathy muttered murderously, turning away from Had to scan what little could be seen of the beach.

"Never is. 'Ceptin' Miz Linzay or yer granddad."

Cathy swung sharply around to face him. "You mean Fin."

"I mean yer granddad." Had picked up the sack and flung it over his shoulder. "Many's the time while workin' on the geranium bed 'neath the winder I've seen 'im sittin' in 'is chair havin' a pipe."

"Had." Cathy spoke his name emphatically. "Ghosts do not smoke pipes. They wear old sheets and moan."

"Wouldn't know." He grasped the sack in both hands and started toward the toolshed. "Never seen a ghost m'self. Jest seen yer granddad."

"Now wait a minute." Cathy scurried after him. "Are you sure you've seen Granddad, not—"

"Yoo-hoo, Hadley!" Cat came out of the greenhouse then, a soil-stained canvas apron tied over her denim coveralls. "What do you think for a border around the patio? Verbena or dianthus? Oh, hello, darling girl!" A delighted smile lit her face as she took in Cathy's nail pouch and dirty hands. "Oh, you've fixed the shutters! Aren't you wonderful! Phineas absolutely hates the sun hitting him in the face when he's trying to write."

Cathy groaned and closed her eyes. When she opened them, Cat had tilted her head to one side and pursed her lips.

"But you've overdone it, haven't you, darling girl?" She tsked solicitously. "You're pale as a ghost again."

"I'm fine," Cathy snapped. "At least I will be as soon as I get my hands on— I mean, as soon as I speak to Fin. Have you seen him, Grandma?"

"No, not since breakfast." Cat's eyelids narrowed to a sly little slant. "Whatever do you want with Fin?"

It was the end. The living or the dead, depending on your point of view. Cathy clenched her fists and shrieked, "I want to kill him!" Then she tore off toward the house.

"Well, now, Miz Linzay, verbena can't take full sun—"

"Oh, Hadley, not *now*!" Cat cried as Cathy took the patio steps two at a time.

She fell through the Dutch door, grabbed the frame to keep from going over and hung there, panting. Helmut raised an unconcerned eye from the *New Yorker*.

"You look like you just seen a ghost, Cath."

"I wish you people would stop saying that to me!" she cried just as Cat's footfalls scraped across the flagstones behind her.

"Darling girl!" Cat called urgently.

Gulping a breath, Cathy raced up the stairs and along the gallery, into her grandmother's room and through the French doors onto the widow's walk. Next to the redwood chaise stood the telescope, which was powerful enough to give Cat, an amateur stargazer, a clear view of Jupiter.

Dropping to her knees, Cathy trained the lens on the dunes. She fumbled and blurred the focus, finally got it right and began a slow sweep of the beach.

"Darling girl!" Cat gasped breathlessly behind her. "What in God's name has— What in hell are you doing now?"

"Looking for Fin," she replied between clenched teeth. "And when I find him I'm going to kill him."

"But why?"

"Because—" Cathy pivoted on one knee, her elbow bumping the telescope and swiveling it a hundred and eighty degrees on its tripod "—he has a lousy sense of humor."

"Absolutely, but that's hardly grounds for murder!"

Cathy just snarled, turned back to the telescope, saw that it was now sighted on the road to Edgartown and swung it back toward the beach.

She'd screwed up the lens. Cursing under her breath she readjusted it. It cleared, bringing the coast road into clear focus just as a fast-moving crimson speck came into range of the lens and took shape as the most distinctive Lincoln Continental ever custom-built by Detroit.

The body was two-tone: scalding pink over scarlet; the landau roof leathered in silver, and it belonged to— No. Oh, God, please, this couldn't be the source of her unease, her foreboding. It couldn't be the Mayflower.

Wiping a hand over her eyes, Cathy looked again through the eyepiece, moving the telescope to bring the Lincoln into focus, then she shrieked, leaped for the French doors and flung her arms around Cat.

"Oh, God, Grandma! It's Aunt Patsy!"

"Where?" Cat pushed her away and scurried toward the telescope. "Show me!"

With shaking fingers, Cathy sighted the lens. Cat bent over and peered into the eyepiece.

"Damn that umbrella!" She grabbed Cathy's elbow and towed her into the house. "We haven't a moment to lose! He-ell-mmuu-tt!"

He met them, glowering, at the foot of the stairs.

"Where's the fire this time?"

"On the road. Patsy—burning up the pavement!"

"I'll get the cigars." Helmut heaved his bulk through the kitchen door faster than Cathy had ever seen him move.

"Quick!" Cat gave her a shove. "Get Hadley and tell him to move it!"

Cathy didn't question, just did it, shrieking at Had from the patio. He dropped the hose he held and came on the fly. Cat and Helmut were both puffing cigars when Cathy and Had came running into the dining room.

"Here!" Cat jammed hers into Cathy's mouth. "Smoke!"

Now she understood. Patsy suffered from every allergy known to man and a few others she'd invented. She was especially sensitive to cigar smoke.

"Fan out!" Cat ordered between drags on a second cigar. "Stink up the whole place!"

They split in four different directions, each one puffing like bellows on Helmut's fat, nasty cigars. Within seconds Cathy's eyes were streaming tears; Had was turning green. Cat had folded up on the window seat. Only Helmut was enjoying himself.

"Enough!" Cat lifted the sheer panel on the window. "Here she—oh, heaven help us!—here they come!"

Helmut appeared with a huge ceramic ashtray, took the cigars and disappeared into the kitchen with Had. Bending one knee on the window seat behind Cat, Cathy looked out the window to watch Mellody disembark the Mayflower.

She'd streaked her blond hair since Cathy had last seen her, and wore designer jeans, a red silk blouse tied at the waist and white snakeskin boots. A pair of designer sunglasses perched on her nose, yet she shaded her eyes with one scarlet sculpture-nailed hand as she walked around the car and leaned against the grill waiting for her mother. Eyeing Mellody's well-endowed chest, Cathy wished she hadn't thrown away the voodoo doll.

"Oh, God, there she is." Cat groaned as the driver's door sprang open. "The one failure of my life."

Her aunt was more beautiful than Cathy remembered, the image of Cat in her prime. Physically anyway, as her father had been fond of pointing out. Her auburn hair was drawn back in a lavender scarf that matched the expensive suit she wore, and her exquisite redhead's skin was flawlessly made up. She met Mellody, slung her arm through hers and they came toward the house.

"Here's how we shall play the scene," Cat said quickly. "We will be surprised—naturally, since the brat never phones, she just appears—but thrilled to see them. I shall offer the Green Rooms but they will decline since within five minutes Patricia will be unable to draw a breath. They'll take the guest cottage instead.

"Probably she wants money—but I wonder since Mellody is with her. Hmm. But with any luck, I shall be able to write her a fat check and we'll be rid of them by morning. If they linger, however, I shall have to rely on you to find out what she's up to. I cannot, for I must be what my daughter thinks I am—a slightly dim but harmless old hag. Will you do that for me, darling girl?"

"You know I will, Grandma."

"Excellent." Cat gave her fingers a squeeze. "Quickly now, look absorbed!"

When her aunt and her cousin appeared on the porch, Cathy was at the computer and Cat was feigning sleep on the window seat. At the slam of the screen door and a flash of lavender in the foyer, she looked up from the keyboard.

"Yoo-hoo, Mother! Mother?" Patsy stopped in the living room doorway with Mellody beside her. As Cathy scrambled out of her chair, her head turned toward the library.

"Aunt Patsy! Mell!" Cathy forced a delighted smile.

"Oh, it's you." Her tone dismissed Cathy as nothing more than the irritant she'd always been, until Cat stirred and snorted on the window seat. Then the gushing started. "How lovely to see you, dear!" Patsy came to kiss her, made sure the buss landed in midair and pirouetted toward the window seat. "Mother, dearest!"

Sweeping past her, Patsy sank to her knees before Cat, leaving Cathy facing her cousin.

"Another career change?" Mellody asked, poking one of the pouches in the apron Cathy had forgotten to take off. "Or is this the blue-collar look?"

Making a noise she hoped would pass for a laugh, Cathy reached for the apron strings. When she went up to the attic to straighten Captain Croft's trunks, she'd unearth her Barbie dolls. And her grandmother's hat pins.

"Nope, I'm still plying my same old trade. From the look of those boots, I guess you are, too."

"Very funny." Mellody sneered and turned toward the window seat. "Darling girl."

"Patricia! Mellody!" Cat sat up stiffly and pressed her cheek to her daughter's forehead. "What brings my Broadway babies all this way? Is something wrong?"

"No, no. Mellie has a few weeks before her new show starts rehearsals so we drove up for a visit. It's been such an age, Mother!"

"How *delightful!*" Cat drew Mellody onto the window seat and kissed her wetly on the cheek.

"Grandma, darling," she cooed, then turned her head and rolled her eyes.

Cathy tossed her apron on the couch and smiled as the nails jingled in the pouches. Who needed hat pins?

"I hope you can stay for days and days!" Cat cried joyously. "Tell me you can!"

"We'll stay as long as you want us to, Mother."

"Oh, marvelous! Then you'll *never* leave!"

They touched cheeks, then Patsy sneezed and dabbed her nose with a hankie untucked from one sleeve. "Mother, have you let that awful man smoke in your house again?"

"Oh, my dear!" Cat clutched Patsy to her breast. "Oh, I'm so sorry! But it's his only vice, you know, and I had *no idea* you were coming!"

"It's all right, Mother." Patsy broke Cat's stranglehold and signed Mellody toward the door. "My overnight, would you, baby?" Nodding, she quit the window seat and went outside. "I'll be fine in a moment. My allergist has me on the most wonderful new medication."

"Oh, how marvelous!" Cat shot Cathy a panicked look over her daughter's head.

Mellody returned with a small case. Patsy sprang it open, withdrew an inhaler and shot two bursts of foul-smelling stuff into her mouth. Cat made a face and batted the fumes away.

"Ah—" Patsy drew a relaxed breath, moved to a small, petit-point chair beside Cat and dropped the inhaler in her lap. "So how's the book coming along, Cathy?"

"Oh, just fine."

"Do you always get so filthy when you write, dear?"

Cathy glanced down at the paint chips on the front of her blue sweatshirt and the grass stains on the knees of her jeans. "Uh, no, actually I was—"

"Nailing up the library shutters," Cat put in cheerfully. "She knows how Phineas hates to have the sun in his eyes while he's trying to write. Excuse me, darlings, I'll put on the kettle and we'll have tea." She tottered away, and Patsy and Mellody exchanged a look that said, "It's worse than we thought."

Uh-oh, thought Cathy. "Grandma means Fin, of course. Fin McGraw, our houseguest. He's, uh, he's a playwright."

"Is that a nickname?" Patsy queried.

"Yes. Short for Phineas."

"Well, how odd. Another playwright named Phineas."

"It's a small world, Aunt Patsy."

"Yes. And getting smaller all the time."

Mellody came to life on the window seat. "Is he a friend of yours, Cathy?"

"No. He's Grandma's friend."

"Oh." Mellody lost interest.

"It will be just a few minutes, my dears." Cat came back into the room, walking as if she was half-blind, placing each foot carefully. "Come, darling girl, give Grandmama a hand."

"Mother, why are you waiting on us with Helmut—"

"Oh, but he's ill, dear!" Cat gripped Cathy's arm and jerked her toward the kitchen. "We had the most awful storm the other day and he's still out of sorts. Besides—" she leaned on Cathy as if she'd topple over without her support "—moving around is good for my arthritis. One moment!"

"Since when do you have arthritis?" Cathy muttered.

"Shh!" Cat pressed a finger to her lips and, once they were in the kitchen, whispered, "All old people have it, so of course she thinks I do. Also I'm slightly deaf. And the peepers are a bit dim. Don't forget."

"It'll never work."

"Of course it will." Cat picked up a pot holder, the kettle and filled a china pot with boiling water. "No one wants to spend time with a crippled, deaf old bat who can't remember what you said five minutes ago and bores you stiff with stories you've heard a thousand times."

"Sure it'll work." Cathy stretched on her toes to retrieve a footed silver tray from an upper shelf. "With our luck, it'll work as well as the cigar smoke."

"Hmm. Yes." Cat took the tray from her, her lips pursing as she arranged the pot, cups and saucers, spoons and napkins. "We've got to get that inhaler from her and lose it."

"Oh, for heaven's sake, Gran—" She jerked, startled, as Cat slapped a hand over her mouth.

"Do you value my sanity and well-being?"

Cathy sucked a breath through her nose and nodded.

"If she stays here any longer than one night I shall run naked and screaming down the beach! Do you understand? *Naked and screaming.*"

Again Cathy nodded.

"All right." Cat picked up the tray and shoved it in Cathy's hands. "Now—*get that damned inhaler!*"

14

PATSY AND MELLODY were on the couch whispering when Cathy came back to the living room with the tea and Cat on her right arm. She put the tray down on the coffee table, helped her feeble old gran onto the window seat, sat down beside her and smiled at her aunt and her cousin.

"Now tell me, Cathy dear," Patsy said pleasantly, "how is the book coming?"

"Oh, marvelously!" Cat crowed and gave Cathy a shove. "Show them, darling girl! Let my little knickerbockers be the first to read it!"

"It's only six pages. Six very rough pages."

"Oh, nonsense!" Cat shoved her again. "It's wonderful stuff! Wonderful!"

"Yes, Cathy, please." The smile on Patsy's face didn't quite reach her eyes. "I'd love to read it."

"How about tomorrow? Give me a chance to smooth things out and—"

"Oh, writers!" Cat laughed and gave Cathy a third shove that nearly knocked her off the window seat. "Never finished with a book! Why Phineas, and Lindsay, too, will just write something to *death*!"

The sidelong glance Patsy swapped with Mellody brought Cathy to her feet. This was only the second one she'd seen, but already she was sick of these silent, speaking looks between mother and daughter. If she had to play their game to figure out what they meant, then so be it.

"You'll have to read it on the monitor, Aunt Patsy. I haven't connected the printer yet."

"That's fine, dear." She reached into her purse for her glasses and followed Cathy toward the library.

Why does she care about Grandma's memoirs, Cathy wondered, rounding the desk to bring up the file. Unless it's a ploy, or she wants to make sure Grandma doesn't tell the world how old she really is. When the first draft appeared, Cathy cringed and stepped back. "Happy reading."

"Thank you, dear." Patsy laid her hand on the back of her father's chair, turned it on its swivel platform to sit down and froze as the screen door slammed and Fin strolled into the living room.

For half a second Cathy thought it was his resemblance to Phineas that caused the color to drain from her aunt's face, then she saw the black kitten with huge golden eyes and bristled tail curled in the curve of Fin's elbow. Cats were about the only animal, vegetable or mineral on the planet Patsy wasn't allergic to, but she was terrified of them. Simply and abjectly terrified.

After the string of dirty tricks fate had played, it was high time for a gimme. Hoping Patsy's catatonia would last a few more seconds, Cathy rushed Fin.

"Oh, you found her!" She gave Fin an upstage wink Mellody couldn't see. "Come to Mommy, lovey."

He looked bewildered but caught the high sign and kept his mouth shut until Cathy reached for the cat. Then Patsy let out a hackle-raising shriek, so did the kitten and so did Fin as it climbed his chest to tremble on his shoulder.

"A cat! A cat! Oh, my God, get it out of here! Get it out, get it out, get it out!"

The kitten yowled, made a swan dive off Fin's shoulder and shot into the library. Screaming, Patsy climbed backward up the wall, clawing books out of the shelves and sending her father's portrait swinging crazily on its hanger. The cat did a three-sixty, soared across the living room and landed in the middle of the tea service. Cat made a grab for it that missed, and the kitten was off again, cups and spoons and saucers flying like shrapnel behind it.

"Help her!" Cat cried, pointing a finger at Patsy, who was sliding limply down the wall on the verge of fainting.

Cathy rushed to catch her, Cat took off in pursuit of the kitten and Mellody made a beeline for Fin.

Bumping against the bookshelves put brake enough on Patsy's descent for Cathy to catch her arms and ease her the last half foot or so to the floor. By then she was out cold, and limp as an overcooked noodle. The only sound was the cat purring loudly. Too loudly, Cathy realized, stepping over her aunt to turn around.

She should've known. It was Mellody, standing before Fin with her hand splayed on his chest. His plaid shirt was open to his navel, and his head was lowered watching Mellody's fingers graze the bleeding skid marks left by the kitten.

"Poor baby." Mellody dipped the tip of one finger in a deep scratch, raised it to her lips and licked.

Fin's nostrils flared and his eyes glazed. They were both damn lucky the hammer was on the couch.

"Mellody Martin, Fin McGraw." Cathy moved to the library doorway, leaned against it and folded her arms.

Fin leaped like a startled virgin and clutched the front of his shirt over his chest. Mellody made a slow pivot on one snakeskin heel. "You've seen the *Tattler* article, I'm sure. It's the reason we came, you know."

"What business is it of yours?"

"It's as much ours as it is yours, darling girl."

Mellody had her there. Fin, Cathy noticed, was paying silent but rapt attention.

"Where's Uncle Lindsay? Mama expected him to be here."

"He's finishing a play, but he'll be along soon."

Behind them, Patsy moaned; Mellody's gaze shifted unconcernedly toward the sound. Then Cat appeared in the kitchen doorway with Helmut in tow and Mellody's sneer vanished.

"Let's hope it's soon enough," she whispered and sidled past Cathy into the library.

"I'm sorry, darling," said Cat, playing ancient and enfeebled again as she tottered toward them, and Helmut veered into the library. "I tried to catch her, but she's gone to ground somewhere. I've never seen such a wily little cat."

The expression on Fin's face said he had, but he wisely kept his lip zipped. He also buttoned his shirt, hastily, as Helmut came out of the library with a scowl on his face, Patsy in his arms and Mellody hovering behind him.

"There, dear," Cat soothed her granddaughter. "Helmut will take you to the guest cottage and Hadley will bring your luggage. We'll be along to have supper with you. Until we find Lovey and shut her away, it's best to keep your mother in the cottage, don't you think?"

"Oh, yes, Grandma. Thank you." Mellody kissed her cheek and fluttered away with Helmut out the veranda doors.

"How long have Piranha Woman and Barracuda Girl been here?" Fin asked, and though Cathy was still furious with him she laughed.

"Too damn long," Cat said feelingly and embraced him.

His arms went around her gently, but he rubbed his nose playfully in her hair. Cat laughed, then grinned at him.

"First thing in the morning I'm changing my will. I'm leaving everything to you and that wretchedly adorable little feline."

"Shove your will, old woman." Fin grinned back at her, the Irish thicker than usual in his voice. "I'll settle for a year's free acting lessons. Swear to God I thought you'd aged twenty years since breakfast."

Cat preened.

Watching them, Cathy felt like an intruder. Not bitter or envious, just left out. "Where's the kitten?"

"I haven't a clue," Cat replied, unthreading herself from Fin's arms. "Somewhere in the house."

On cue, the missing feline meowed, faintly yet mournfully. Cathy couldn't tell from where.

"Ah." Cat beamed. "Music to my ears."

"Poor thing," Cathy murmured sympathetically. "It's frightened to death."

"Not to worry, he'll come out when he's hungry." Fin glanced her an arch smile. "Lovey is a tom."

It figured.

"I heard Mellody mention the *Tattler*, darling girl. What gives?"

"That's the reason they came, she said. Which I tried to warn you about, but no—"

"Oh, bosh." Cat gave a snort and a dismissive wave.

"She also wanted to know," Fin said, "why Uncle Lindsay isn't here."

"Why in hell did she think he would be?" Cat asked.

Cathy decided it was a good time to clean up the wreck of the tea service. Fin lent a hand, while Cat parked on the window seat, put her hands on her knees and pursed her lips.

Helmut came through the veranda doors, glanced over the quarterdeck rail at Cathy and Fin on the floor and spoke two words. "Club soda." Then he went back to the kitchen.

"I'm going to take a bath." Cat got to her feet and marched up the stairs and along the gallery to her room.

When the door shut behind her, Fin sat back and looked at Cathy. She sat back and looked at him. The hammer lay within easy reach, but she felt no desire to pick it up. She wondered instead what Fin would do if she tore open his shirt and licked the scratches on his chest.

"You called your father, didn't you?"

"Yes."

"If I were you I'd call him again." Fin dumped the last of the broken china on the tray, picked it up and got to his feet. "I've got a bad feeling about all this."

He went into the kitchen, came out and went up the stairs to his room without so much as a glance in her direction. This time Cathy didn't feel left out, she felt shut out. Deliberately and deservedly, she supposed, but painfully nonetheless.

She got up and went into the kitchen for club soda. Helmut stood at the sink cleaning the footed silver tray.

"Did ya get him?"

"No, I chickened out," she said. As usual, she thought.

"Maybe the little man-eater'll finish 'im off."

At the memory of Mellody licking Fin's blood from her finger, Cathy felt like gnawing the cap off the club soda. But she used the bottle opener, and then, because she was standing next to it and it rang, she answered the phone.

"How dare you?" Her mother demanded. "How dare you send Noel down here to do your whining for you! Your father was on the ragged edge anyway, and now he's taken himself and his computer to a hotel! I don't know which one, because he wouldn't tell me. If I knew, I'd tell you, he said, and then he'd never finish the third act."

"Well." Cathy took a deep breath to keep from screaming. "If and when you talk to Daddy dearest, tell him for me, 'Screw the third act.' Aunt Patsy and Mellody are here because of the *Tattler* article he thinks is such a hoot!"

"Oh, God! What does she want?"

"I don't know, I haven't figured it out yet. As for Noel, I did not send him to Boston to whine for me. I'm perfectly capable of whining for myself. I did ask him to stay, but he had a date with his agent and his editor."

"Oh. I shot from the hip, I guess. I'm sorry."

"Apology accepted. Now what do we do?"

"I start calling hotels. You keep one eye on Cat and the other one on Patsy. I'll check with you later."

"All right, Mom. G'bye." Cathy hung up and leaned her shoulder blades against the wall next to the phone. She was thinking about beating her head against it when Helmut half turned away from the sink.

"Hey, Cath—catch." She did and grinned at Patsy's inhaler. "Helmut, you old fox!"

"Don't say I never gave ya nothin'," he growled and turned back to the sink.

Cathy didn't, just put the inhaler in her pocket, swiped up a sponge and went to scrub the rug with the club soda. As she passed through the kitchen doorway the kitten streaked between her legs with something silver and flashy in its mouth and rocketed up the stairs. Dumping the sponge and the soda on the dining room table, Cathy gave chase.

When she turned the corner on the landing, Fin was rising to his feet outside his bedroom door with the cat in his right hand and his left sliding something into the pocket of his gray pleated front trousers. He'd changed into a blue dress shirt, the sleeves rolled to his elbows, and red suspenders. Her grandfather's; she'd know them anywhere.

"Where've you been, old sod? You're filthy." Fin scratched the kitten's dirty ears and glanced at Cathy. "Where'd you find him?"

"I didn't. He came tearing out of the kitchen and I followed." She climbed the rest of the stairs and stroked one hand lightly down the cat's back.

Lovey—she had to find a better name—arched his back and purred. Dust clung to his whiskers and there was a cobweb caught in his tail. Cathy tugged it out, gave him another stroke and felt his ribs beneath his fur.

"What did he have in his mouth?"

"Oh, just this." He shifted the kitten to his other hand and fished a piece of silver foil from the top of a pack of cigarettes out of his pocket. The cat reached for it with a front paw and hooked his claws in Fin's ring finger. "Ouch, ungrateful wretch." He put the kitten and the foil on the floor and watched him bat it around.

It made a nice cat toy, but it wasn't what Cathy had seen in his mouth. Whatever that was, Fin had put in his left pocket, not his right. "Where did you find him?"

"On the beach. He followed me home."

"That's what they all say." Cathy smiled and folded her arms. Inky—nah—rolled on his back and started to eat the foil. "How old is he, d'you think?"

"Three or four months." Fin dropped to his heels, took the foil away from the kitten and scratched his belly. "If Cat keeps him he'll need to be neutered soon or he'll start spraying to mark his territory."

Except for a tiny white—Spot?—on his chest the cat was black as—Midnight?

"Spraying what?"

"You don't want to know."

From his crouch beside Lovey, Fin grinned up at her. With the fabric of his trousers drawn tight, Cathy could see the muscles in his thighs, and the small sharp-edged lump in his left pocket.

"I'll show you what's in my pocket," she said, reaching into her jeans, "if you'll show me what's in yours."

"Which pocket?" Fin asked, stretching to his feet.

"Left," she answered, producing the inhaler on her flattened palm. "The breath of Piranha Woman's allergy-riddled life, compliments of Helmut."

"That sly old boots." Fin laughed, dipping his hand in his pocket. "Ready?"

"I'm tingling with anticipation."

"At long last." He held out his hand and his car keys.

"Nothing else?"

"Which pocket?" Fin grinned.

Cathy made a face at him, and realized they weren't shouting or hurling insults at each other. Loath as she was to break the fragile peace between them, or antagonize him any further, she had to ask, "How old are you, Fin?"

"Twenty-seven in August," he said, stepping toward her.

Her grandfather had died six months before he was born. That was certainly immediate, and there was no doubting the physical likeness. The temperament Cathy wasn't sure about. Fin had a temper as Irish as his accent, but she hadn't a clue about Phineas; she'd never asked. By her own admission, Cat was trying to make a playwright out of Fin, but that didn't necessarily mean she thought he was Phineas reborn. Or did it?

"You don't mind that I'm a tad younger than you?"

"Why should I?"

"No reason. Just wondered." He took another step toward her and smiled. "Since I'm rapidly approaching being over the hill, you'd better hurry and snatch me up."

Better snatch *me* up, Cathy thought, before I ask about your beach house. Just then Cat's bedroom door opened, and she stepped out onto the gallery in pastel blue knit slacks, a white turtleneck and a cardigan banded in blue and coral. She appeared to have shrunk two inches under the weight of the ropes, chains, bracelets and rings she wore. Cat loved jewelry, wore tons of it always, but this was the real stuff, not costume.

"Anyone seen the newest addition to the family?" she asked as she came toward them.

Both Fin and Cathy looked down. The kitten was gone.

"Where'd he go?" Cathy asked Fin. "He was here just a second ago."

"It would seem," he replied with a chuckle, "we have an escape artist in our midst."

"That's it!" Cathy grinned. "The perfect name for him—Houdini!"

"Houdini," he repeated and nodded. "I like it."

"Then Houdini it is," Cat decreed, stopping beside Fin and looping her hand through his elbow.

"Overdoing it, aren't you?" Cathy asked.

"I certainly hope so." Cat's grin outshone the glittering stones she wore. "It drives Patricia mad when I parade the family jewels."

She wagged her eyebrows at Fin. He held his nose and groaned, but he couldn't take his eyes off the fortune draped around Cat's neck. Cathy calculated she was wearing a cool twenty-five thousand worth of baubles.

"Why do you bait her, Grandma?"

"Because it's fun, darling girl, and because, even though she's a royal pain in the ass, I'm her mother and I love her and I keep trying to save her from herself."

"This is going to save her?"

"No. Mostly this is just fun. She'll all but drown in her own drool. Now shake a leg, darling girl, we have to take them supper and be sociable." With her free hand, Cat lifted an opera-length pearl rope and regarded it thoughtfully. "Maybe I can buy her off with this."

So much for saving Aunt Patsy, Cathy thought, shaking her head as she went to change her clothes.

15

THE SALIVATING STARTED as soon as Patsy laid eyes on her mother and Mellody laid eyes on Fin. The wheedling and whining about Houdini didn't start until after they'd polished off one of Helmut's epicurean picnic hampers.

"I'm not asking you to destroy it, Mother," Patsy claimed, although Cathy didn't like the gleam in her eyes, "just get rid of it."

"But Patricia, dear," Cat replied, waving a hand around the living room. "Aren't you comfortable here?"

Cleopatra would have felt at home in the posh little two-bedroom cottage. It rivaled the Beverly Hills Hotel, where Patsy always stayed when she worked in L.A., and had once been featured in a six-page layout in *House Beautiful*.

"That's not the point, Mother," she argued. "The point is Mellody and I belong in the house where we can spend more time with you, and that wretched creature doesn't."

"That wretched creature *lives* in the house," Cat retorted, her rickety old-fogy facade slipping along with her patience. "Houdini has been abused and abandoned and I will not further damage his psyche by confining him."

The gauntlet was thrown. Patsy and Mellody exchanged a look across the coffee table that clearly said, "Get that damn cat."

"I thought the cat's name was Lovey," Mellody said, her eyes narrowing suspiciously.

"Oh, that's just a pet name," Cathy replied quickly.

Fin rolled his eyes.

"Obviously, Mother," Patsy said petulantly, "that vile animal means more to you then Mellody and I."

"Since you bring it up—"

"Ready for strawberries and whipped cream?" Cathy sprang to her feet with a cheerfully toothy smile.

"Thank you, dear." Patsy glared at her. "In a moment."

"Yes, darling girl." Cat, sagging back into character, gave her a vague and myopic smile. "That would be lovely."

"I'll give you a hand." Fin followed her to the glass-topped dinette table and muttered in her ear. "We'd better get Cat out of here before she loses it altogether."

"Right after dessert," she whispered back.

Fin carried three crystal compotes back to the living room, gave one to Patsy, kept one, gave the other to Mellody and sat down in the chair next to hers. Mellody dipped her middle finger in the cream, licked it off and smiled.

"I read the most fascinating article in *Cosmo*," she said to Fin. "How Whipped Cream Can Save Your Marriage."

Fin gurgled. Before Cathy could throw them, Cat took one of the two compotes Cathy held, grabbed her elbow and tugged her down on the couch.

Five minutes later, claiming it was time for her blood-pressure pill, Cat put aside her dish and rose. So did Fin and Cathy. Good-night kisses were exchanged, the only heartfelt one in the room the lip sucker Mellody clamped on Fin. It left him dazed and shaking. The flashlight beam trembled in his grip all the way up the driveway and the patio steps.

"I need a cigarette," Cat declared as she swept through the Dutch door.

"I need a drink," Cathy muttered behind her.

Fin just smiled and put the hamper down on the counter. Cathy wanted to bean him with it, but mixed herself a screwdriver instead, and stuck her head into Helmut's room.

"Seen the cat lately?"

He raised his head from the book on his lap, one of the Conan Doyle volumes, Cathy thought. "He's been in the kitchen a couple times to eat and use his litter box. Had jury-rigged one outta an old dishpan and some sand."

"I'll buy him a real one tomorrow and some cat food."

"Nah. He likes smoked salmon all right."

Houdini yowled then from somewhere, a low, pitiful meow.

"Where does he keep going off to?" Cathy asked.

"In this house? You gotta be kiddin'."

He went back to his book, and Cathy went to the living room.

Fingers laced on his chest, Fin sprawled on the couch staring at the ceiling. The brass floor lamp was on, illuminating the driftwood tiger on the mantel, and the window seat where Cat sat puffing pensively.

The wreath of blue smoke drifting around her shoulders made Cathy's mouth water. She hadn't had a cigarette in two days, not since she'd whacked her head on the saber-tooth. Helping herself to one from Cat's pack, Cathy sat down next to her and lit it with a pink disposable lighter.

The first drag gave her a rush and made her head swim. It was divine, orgasmic—and so was the simmering sidelong glance Fin gave her bare legs as she crossed them at the knee. They weren't her best feature, but she'd worn a midcalf, clingy silk print skirt and mauve camp shirt to compete with Mellody's snakeskin boots.

"Whatever Patsy has come for is in this house," Cat said, more to herself, Cathy thought, than anyone else.

"Based on the fit she threw over Houdini, I'd say that's a lead-pipe cinch," she agreed. "What d'you suppose it is?"

"I haven't the foggiest." Cat sighed heavily, put out her cigarette and gave Cathy's hand a grateful squeeze. "Thank you, darling, for coming to my rescue. I can't believe I allowed her to provoke me into breaking character."

Now her grandmother's distraction made sense. Cathy slipped a consoling arm around her shoulders.

"Nor can I believe I didn't make her take all her negative energy with her when she left." Cat shuddered. "Can you feel it, darling girl?"

"No, can't say that I do," Cathy said slowly, taking a quick swig of her screwdriver. What she could feel was Fin's gaze sliding down her legs to linger on her ankles.

"No matter. I shall meditate and get rid of it." Cat patted her wrist and rose. She lit the candles in the holders on both sides of the saber-tooth, the score or so more scattered on tables around the room and switched off the floor lamp. "Let these burn awhile, will you? They'll cleanse the room."

Then she went upstairs, leaving Cathy and Fin gazing at each other across the candlelit room. He rolled on his side to face her, bent his elbow and put his head in his hand. The candle flames flickered in his eyes and gleamed on Cathy's smooth calves.

"Make me the happiest man on earth," he said. "Tell me nymphomania runs in your family." She laughed and Fin smiled. "Better yet, come over here and show me."

Cathy put her cigarette out, her drink on the floor and went. From the corner of her eye as she rose to her feet, she could've sworn she saw a dazzling spiral of light emanating from the tiger, but she ignored it.

She ignored everything but the glow in Fin's eyes and the flare of his nostrils as she sat down beside him and undid the top two buttons of her shirt. He unfastened two more and pulled her down beside him, slid his left hand behind her to cradle her head and his right beneath her skirt to lift her knee and press himself between her legs.

The phone rang and they both groaned.

"Did you talk to your father?"

"No, he's gone to a hotel. Mom's trying to find him."

"So that could be her."

The phone continued to ring.

"Yes."

"Then you'd better answer it." Fin sighed and rolled her away from him.

On shaky knees, Cathy hurried to the kitchen wall phone, picked it up and said, "Hello."

"No luck. How about you?"

"Aunt Patsy's after something in the house," Cathy said and told her about Houdini.

"The cat should buy us some time, then." Her mother sighed. "Have you heard from Noel?"

"No."

"He called here to see how things are going. I told him Patsy was there, and he said he'd get back to the Vineyard as soon as he could."

"Where was he?"

"New York, I assume. He's not meeting his agent until tomorrow. His editor had to cancel tonight."

"Why did he call you? Why didn't he call me?"

"He hoped your father would answer, I think. He asked to speak to him, and I told him he'd gone to a hotel."

"And you haven't heard from Dad?"

"No, but I'll call you as soon as I do."

"All right, Mother. Good night."

The window over the sink was open a crack to let in the cool spring evening. A breath of wind stirred the curtains and chilled her overheated skin. She hung up the phone and reached for the buttons as she started back to the living room, smiling and shivering with anticipation at the thought of letting Fin undo them again.

When she came through the kitchen door, he was waiting for her at the foot of the stairs with one of the candles. "Don't fasten them," he said softly and held out his hand.

Cathy's fingers slipped away from the buttons and wound through his. The steps creaked as Fin led her upstairs. Outside his door she hesitated, her gaze sliding down the gallery to Cat's room.

"She'll be all right for a couple of hours," Fin said gently. "And I don't think she'll mind if I make love with her granddaughter in her house."

"No, she won't mind at all." Cathy smiled at him. "But lock the door or she'll be in here giving us pointers."

Laughing, Fin did so, then he drew Cathy to the bed, put the candle on the nightstand, sat her on the edge of the mattress and got down on his knees between hers. While he unfastened her last two buttons, Cathy undid his shirt. With her fingertips she found the scratches left by the cat's claws, bent her head and kissed them.

Fin groaned and curved one hand around the nape of her neck. "Oh, pussy willow," he murmured into her hair.

Touching her lips to his collarbone, Cathy raised her head and looked into his eyes. "Why d'you call me that?"

"Because that's what you looked like when I found you on the beach wrapped up in the quilt." Fin slid her shirt off, tugged her camisole free of her waistband and slipped his hands beneath it. "My very own little pussy willow."

His thumbs slid up her rib cage, grazed the undersides of her breasts, then he lowered his mouth and gently sucked her left nipple into his mouth. The friction of the silk camisole and his probing tongue against her nipple created a delicious ache. Cathy laced her fingers behind his head, pulled him closer and buried her face in his hair.

Thump . . . thump . . . thump . . .

Was that her heart or Fin's? she wondered dazedly as his mouth moved to her right nipple. He nibbled first, wetting the silk with his tongue, and Cathy moaned.

Thump . . . thump . . . thump . . .

No. It wasn't her heart. Or Fin's. It was—

"Grandma!" she gasped.

"Shh. I don't think so." Fin kissed the hollow of her throat and turned his head to listen.

Thump . . . thump . . . thump . . .

Now Cathy recognized the sounds. "It's that damn raven!" she swore, balling her fists on the edge of the mattress. "Well, now hear this, buster— *Nevermore!*" She started to rise, but Fin held her on the bed.

"What raven? What are you talking about?"

"Those noises we heard the other night?" Cathy asked, and Fin nodded. "Noel heard them, too. Rather, one of Grandma's other coauthors did, and described them to Noel as a 'rapping at my chamber door' like in *The Raven*."

Thump . . . thump . . . thump . . .

"Really?" Fin said thoughtfully and got to his feet, lifting and kissing Cathy's hands. "I'm going to take a quick look around."

"I'm coming with you."

"No." He leaned over and kissed her lingeringly. "Don't move," he whispered. "Stay here and think about what you want me to kiss when I come back."

"That's easy. Every inch of me."

"You wanton." Fin chuckled huskily, dropped a quick kiss on her nose and slipped out the door.

Sighing and stretching luxuriantly, Cathy flung out her arms and lay on her back. Her knuckles brushed something warm and purring. She turned her head and saw Houdini curled near the foot of the bed, his black fur and slitted gold eyes gleaming in the candlelight.

"Why, you little voyeur." She chuckled.

Yawning Houdini stretched up on his back legs and kneaded his front paws in the bedspread. His claws snagged and lifted the chenille, spilling into Cathy's upturned palm the emerald-and-diamond earring he'd been lying on. The stones sparkled and winked in the candlelight, just as the saber-tooth had winked at her from the mantel. Cathy's fingers turned to ice as she sat up with the earring.

Recalling the dazzled look in Fin's eyes, how he hadn't been able to tear his gaze away from Cat in her finery, she wondered if he knew about the wall safe behind the seascape over her grandmother's bed. Did he know the jewelry inside, gifts from her grandfather, rivaled the Duchess of Windsor's collection?

Shaking and feeling sick, Cathy laid the earring down long enough to put on her shirt, button it and switch on the lamp. She shook out the bedspread, felt under the pillows and all around the edges of the mattress, and had just opened the drawer in the nightstand when Fin came back.

"What are you looking for, Cath?"

She turned to face him, holding the earring aloft in her thumb and forefinger. "My grandmother's other earring."

"That isn't Cat's," he replied curtly.

"Well, it sure as hell isn't mine."

He stood looking at her for a moment, then opened the door he'd just shut and locked. "I've had enough of this." He crossed the room in two strides, grasped Cathy's wrist and pulled her out onto the gallery.

She couldn't break his hold, but she did manage to dig in her heels and wrench him around to look at her. "Just make up an excuse and leave. I don't want to hurt her."

"Oh, that's rich coming from you." Fin laughed unpleasantly and jerked her forward.

Again Cathy pulled back on her wrist and turned him around. "What's that supposed to mean?"

"It means how many times in the past nine years beyond her birthday and Christmas did you give a single thought to her?" Fin stabbed an index finger at Cat's closed door. "I can tell you exactly because I was here—never." Cathy's left hand came up to slap him, but he caught her wrist and held it fast. "While you and the next Olivier were off doing your Lunt and Fontaine imitations, I listened to her stories, I took her for walks on the beach—"

"You want a medal?" Cathy cut in angrily.

"No. I want you to understand that I smiled when she told the same story a hundred times, and walked a little slower so she could keep up with me, because I love her. Not for who she is or what she can do for me, but simply because she's the most extraordinary person I've ever known. If she were thirty years younger I'd have married her."

At last Fin raised his voice. Not much, but enough to make Cathy realize she'd really put her foot in it this time. If the earring belonged to Cat, he wouldn't be dragging her down the gallery to her room; if he hadn't meant what he said he would've screamed and shouted, because it wouldn't matter whether she'd heard him or not. But it had mattered, and Fin did care. That's why he'd spoken each word in that deadly calm voice, because he hadn't wanted her to miss a single syllable.

"Why didn't you tell me this before?" Cathy demanded.

"When did you give me the chance? When would you have listened?"

"I don't know," she replied truthfully, "but you could at least have given me a shot at it."

"Maybe so. I'll give you that."

"You're right, I've been neglectful, I've already realized it—I don't need you to tell me. It may not seem like it to you, but I love my grandmother very, very much."

"That's what really tears it." Fin's grip on her wrist eased a bit. "All Cat talks about is her darling girl. I know everything there is to know about you, because she told me. I thought you were wonderful. I couldn't wait to meet you. I was already half in love with you before you came."

And with that, he dragged a stunned Cathy the rest of the way along the gallery, rapped on her grandmother's door and flung it open when she trilled, "Come in!"

Cat sat Indian-style on her bed, a white candle burning in a brass holder on the nightstand. She was smiling, her half lenses perched on her nose, the red leather book open in her lap. Realizing she was about to wipe the smile off her grandmother's face, Cathy tried to twist free of Fin, but he gave a last tug on her wrist that whipped her into the room as if she'd been shot from a sling.

"Your granddaughter," he said tersely, "has something she believes belongs to you."

"Oh?" Cat took off her glasses and laid them aside on top of the book. "What is it, darling girl?"

"A mistake," Cathy said shakily. "A dreadful, stupid mistake." Then she cast an imploring look at Fin.

He gazed back at her for a moment, then sighed heavily. "Oh, to hell with it. I'm too bloody tired. I haven't had a decent night's sleep in two days." He raked a hand through his hair, then glanced at Cat. "I'm going home. It's lousy timing, I know, but . . ."

"Why?" Cat unfolded her legs and swung herself off the bed. "What's happened? What's going on?"

"You know where I am if you need me," Fin went on, ignoring her question. "You might consider booting Houdini into the basement or the attic for a while. If you let her into the house, Patsy might give you some clue to what it is she wants."

"I'll consider it. Are you going now?"

"Yes. See you on the beach in the morning, though. Around eight?"

"Eight it is." Cat nodded and followed him to the door.

Cathy took a tentative, hopeful step with her, but Fin ignored her, raised a hand to touch her grandmother's cheek and left. Cat shut the door and turned around.

"Explain."

Cathy did, from the beginning. She told Cat about the shack, the Jeep, what she'd thought about Fin, what she'd theorized. She told her everything and wanted to die, because saying it made her sound like the spoiled, rich little brat Fin had said she was.

"Let me see the earring, please." Cat held out her hand and Cathy gave it to her. She examined it for a moment, turned it over in her palm, held it up to the light, then fixed an icy gaze on Cathy. "This isn't mine, which you would have realized had you taken the time to examine it. It's quite old, I'm sure. I've never seen anything like it. Where did Fin find it?"

"I—I don't know," Cathy stammered. "I didn't ask."

"You didn't? Why ever— Oh, *silly* me!" Cat fluttered her fingers and stalked past her toward the bed. "Why, of course, there was no need to ask!"

Cathy whirled after her. "That isn't fair, Grandma!"

"Of course it isn't fair!" Cat snatched up her backrest and threw it across the room. "But it's what you deserve for assuming that because I'm old I'm too stupid to realize when I've been taken in by a handsome face!"

"I didn't—" Cathy started, then stopped. She'd implied it, and heaven help her, she'd thought it. Never believed it, but she'd thought it. "I'm sorry, Grandma."

"I'd like you to leave now." Cat turned away from her and tugged her nightgown out from under her pillow. "I've nothing more to say to you and I'm very tired."

She flung back the bedspread with such force that her book and her glasses tumbled onto the floor. Cathy picked them up and held them out to her.

"You dropped these," she said, but Cat ignored her and started to undress.

Her eyes filling with tears, Cathy put them on the foot of the bed and turned toward her room.

"Oh, there is one more thing."

"Yes?" Cathy gave a hopeful smile over her shoulder.

Cat stuck her arms into the flannel sleeves, pulled the gown over her head and told her, "You're fired."

16

AT 8:00 A.M. Cathy was on the widow's walk when Cat, pink-and-white umbrella in hand, embarked on her morning stroll along the beach. She wore a flaming-red sweater so she'd be sure to be seen, but neither Cat nor Fin, who waited at the end of the boardwalk, deigned to so much as glance in her direction. They simply meandered away as if they hadn't a care in the world.

Clearly they intended to fight dirty. But that was okay, because so did Cathy. Smiling, she went inside, drank two cups of coffee and called her mother.

"Have you found Dad yet?"

"No, I haven't," she snapped. Cathy wasn't the only nonmorning person in the family. "I told you I'd call when I do."

"Forget it, Mom. Leave Dad and his third act, wherever they are, be. I can take care of things without him."

"What things are we talking about?"

"Anything and everything that comes down the pike."

"Cathy," her mother asked suspiciously, "have you been out in the sun without a hat?"

"No," she replied cheerfully. "I've been slapped in the face, kicked in the teeth, insulted, humiliated, defamed, slandered and told I'm not a very nice person."

"Oh. Well, don't take it personally. Helmut treats everybody that way."

"So go shopping or something, Mother. I can handle things here."

"You're sure?"

"Absolutely. I'll call you, well, sometime soon."

"Okay," her mother said slowly and hung up the phone.

Cathy drank more coffee and paced and fidgeted in her room until 10:07, when she was sure her grandmother would be in the greenhouse. She was, in her coveralls and canvas apron, sitting on a three-legged stool at the potting bench piddling with her hydrangeas. When Cathy hied herself onto the bench and leaned the heels of her hands on the splintered edge, Cat ignored her.

"You can't fire me, Grandma."

Cat made no reply, just continued pressing soil around the roots of the freshly potted hydrangeas.

"You can't fire me," Cathy repeated, "because I quit."

Still no reply. Screaming and railing and name-calling she could deal with; being treated like an untouchable was driving her nuts. Not that she didn't deserve it, but . . .

A stack of dirty flats and muddy trowels lay at the far end of the bench. Cathy filled a dented aluminum bucket at the inside spigot and attacked them with a wire brush. It took forever to scrape off the cementlike mud, but finally they were clean. She put the trowels back in the rack built to hold them, and at last Cat looked up at her.

"You changed your room," she said.

Overhauled was a better word. Sometime around 3:00 a.m., Cathy had realized that sobbing her heart out would only earn her another headache and puffy eyes, that it wouldn't do a damn thing to win back Cat's and Fin's love and respect. So she'd savaged her room of anything and everything that smacked of adolescence.

The playbills were gone and so were the posters. To hide the clean rectangles they'd left on the walls, she'd replaced them with baby quilts she'd found in the attic in a trunk marked Lindsay. The only thing she'd kept was Snoopy.

"It was way past time, don't you think?" When Cat made no reply, she went on. "I'm surprised you didn't hear me. I must've been in and out of the attic a dozen times, plus I rearranged the furniture twice."

"It looks very nice. Very chic, but—" Cat paused, and so did her muddy fingers on the root ball of a white hydrangea "—very different."

"I'm different, Grandma. I grew up." Cathy leaned her right hip against the bench and faced her. "I'm sorry I didn't grow up perfect, but frankly, I've yet to run across anybody who did. Well, maybe Dad. But he's not the point, the point is—"

"I know what the point is." Cat pushed her stool away from the bench and turned it toward Cathy. "Oh, darling girl, I'm so sorry!" She threw her arms wide and Cathy slipped into them and hugged her fiercely.

"This is all my fault." Cat took Cathy's hands and held them tightly to her bosom. "I got you off on the wrong foot with Fin, but I thought it would be so *romantic*, you see, to send you off for the tiger and have you find this gorgeous man instead. I never *dreamed* you'd think he was Phineas!"

"It wasn't that bad an idea. And it isn't fair to hog all the blame since there's plenty to go around. Fin deserves a fair share for not owning up to the A-frame."

"Silly man." Cat made a face. "I advised him to tell you straight off, make a clean breast of it, but no . . ."

"Tell me what? About the wife and kids?"

"Oh, no, nothing like that." Cat laughed. "Of course he didn't, and then we were stuck with it. But it did occur to me that having him underfoot might, well, move things along a bit faster, so—"

"Uh-huh," Cathy put in with a smirk.

"Is it wrong of me to want you to be happy?"

"No, Grandma, but it's my life and my choice."

Cat looked down her nose at her. "Considering your first choice, is it any wonder I thought you needed help?"

"Well, since you put it like that . . ."

There was a thump against the side of the greenhouse. They started and turned to look at Houdini, clinging by his claws to the narrow outside ledge between the concrete-block foundation and the windows. Back arched, nose pressed to the filtered glass, he mouthed a meow they couldn't hear.

"Patsy!" Cat gasped, then flung out her arm and cried, "Look there!"

Cathy did, and saw the Mayflower rolling down the driveway. There was room to park four cars abreast in front of the garage, but the Lincoln came to rest squarely behind her MG. A moment later, Mellody got out from behind the wheel. Appropriately she wore her snakeskin boots and cast a satisfied smile at the cat rubbing along the greenhouse ledge.

"Stay here," Cathy said and made for the door.

"Like hell!" Cat slid off the stool and hurried after her. "It's *my* house she's invaded!"

"Remember what Fin said?" Cathy turned in the doorway and laid her hands on her grandmother's shoulders. "If we let her into the house she might tip her hand? Let's try it. Give me five minutes, then bring in Houdini."

"Five minutes it is." Cat held up a finger, then ducked around the side of the greenhouse. "Here, kitty kitty. . ."

Resolving to be a forceful person had sounded so simple at 3:00 a.m. So simple that Cathy had actually hungered for a challenge, never imagining it would come so quick, or that it would come in the guise of Piranha Woman.

Her knees were quaking as she opened the Dutch door and stepped into the back hall. Helmut was in his morris chair, a Conan Doyle volume upside down in his lap, a thunderous scowl on his face.

"The cat okay?" he asked.

"He's fine. Why?"

"The little man-eater drop-kicked him off the veranda."

"I'll drop-kick her," Cathy muttered, remembering the viciously pointed toes of Mellody's boots.

Helmut stretched to his feet. "Need any help?"

It was tempting, oh so tempting. "No, I'll handle her."

Surprise flickered across his face, then he grinned. "'Atta girl." He sat down and turned his book right side up. "She's in the living room."

So was Cathy's cassette recorder, on the window seat beside Patsy, whose head was bent over Cat's red leather copy of *We've Been Here Before*. The book had been on her grandmother's nightstand and the recorder had been on her dresser. Realizing that either her aunt or Mellody had tossed her bedroom and Cat's stopped her shakes. And made her mad.

"I'd have loaned that to you if you'd asked," Cathy said from the gap in the quarterdeck rail. "But since you rifled my room to get it, I want it back."

Her aunt didn't even start, just looked up at her with a smile, her sapphire eyes flicking over Cathy's dirty hands and the mud-spattered front of her red cable-knit sweater. Patsy wore designer jeans, expensive sneakers and a snowy silk blouse. "Every time I see you you're filthy. Why is that?"

"Give that back to me, Aunt Patsy."

"In a moment." She hit the play button and shifted on the window seat to look at Cathy.

"'She hated me, I can tell you. Darling girl, will you promise me something? If I speak to Phineas and he's willing to whip up something for you, will you take it—'"

Oh, God, Cathy moaned silently, realizing Patsy was watching for a reaction. Don't blink, she told herself, don't move, don't even breathe.

Patsy hit the Stop/Eject button, took out the tape, rose and held the recorder out to Cathy. "Here you are, dear."

"I need that tape for the book, Aunt Patsy."

"I need it, too. For evidence."

"Evidence of what?"

"That Mother is senile and no longer competent to handle her own affairs." She laid the tape on the book and folded them both protectively in the crook of her arm. "I've been terribly worried about her for quite some time. When Noel called me—"

"Noel!" Cathy cried, thunderstruck.

"Yes. He called when Lindsay, the pompous ass, refused to listen to him. Since I shared his concerns for Mother's well-being, of course I listened."

"Oh, I'll just bet you did."

"Don't take that tone of voice with me." Patsy's fingers turned white on the red leather binding. "I don't happen to think you're as adorable as Mother does."

"You'll be thrown out of court on your ear with that tape. It's incriminating only out of context."

"'A soul abruptly parted from the body,'" she replied smugly, quoting from *We've Been Here Before*, "'...tends to reincarnate almost immediately. Such souls tend to seek out a body of like appearance, temperament and capability to fulfill their karmic purpose.' Does that sound rational to you? It put me in mind of your young man, who looks remarkably like my father."

"I told you he was a playwright, Aunt Patsy. Fin McGraw is the Phineas Grandma was referring to on the tape."

"I think that's best determined by a judge."

"Surely you can't be stupid enough to take just those two flimsy bits of evidence into a courtroom."

"You're forgetting the article in the *National Tattler*, and the 'sources close to Catherine Lindsay.' I intend to subpoena all eight of them to testify to my mother's irrational behavior."

"Noel won't. And I can't believe even you would do such a thing."

"Believe it," she snapped and stopped smiling.

"And to think," Cathy said with a slow shake of her head, "that I used to feel sorry for you."

"You don't know the meaning of the word, but you'll find out when I'm Mother's legal guardian and I control your trust fund until your thirtieth birthday." Patsy's face flushed unbecomingly in uneven patches. "Then let's see Mother and Lindsay pat me on the head and tell me to go away like a good little girl!"

Neither Phineas nor Lindsay Martin could have written a better stage direction than Houdini soaring over the back of the sofa to land in Cathy's arms. Patsy shrieked, threw the book one way, the tape the other and went hurtling out the front door.

"Flawless as ever," Cathy said, turning to grin at the couch.

"Thank you." Cat popped up behind it and swept her a florid bow. "Impeccable timing has always been a hallmark of my performance."

"How much of that did you hear?"

"Enough." Cat shuddered, then beamed. "You were marvelous! Saint Joan of Arc vanquishing the heathen English!"

"Saint Houdini of Cat, you mean. And I've got a feeling it's only a temporary vanquish."

"Pooh!" Cat snorted and came around the quarterdeck rail into the living room. "What can she do? Stir up more gossip? Who cares! Drag me to court? Let her! The judge will throw her out on her ear, just as you said."

Me and my big mouth, Cathy thought dismally.

"It's your cue, darling." Cat put her hands on her hips. "Time to deliver your impassioned speech to rally the troops, to instill them with hope and courage in the face of overwhelming—" Her voice broke and she folded abruptly onto the couch, her eyes swimming with tears. "Dear God. What have I done to make her hate me so much?"

Cathy gently dumped Houdini on the floor, sat beside Cat and swept her arms around her.

"She doesn't hate you, Grandma, she hates herself. She thinks she has to tear you down to build herself up."

"Yes, I got that impression. Do you remember, darling, when I told you if I could survive being called 'Lindsay the whore' I could survive anything?"

"Yes, Grandma, I remember."

"Well," Cat continued, tremulously and wiping a tear off her chin. "I may have been wrong."

17

BY THE TIME Cathy reached Fin's A-frame, she had sand in her sneakers, grit up her nose, and dirty knuckles. She noticed the mud from the trowels when she raised her hand to knock on the smoked-glass atrium doors that opened onto the deck, and tried to rub it off while she waited for Fin to answer. She tried to catch her breath, too, but she was panting like a wind-broken horse when he opened the left-hand door.

"Gimme—a minute—" Cathy gasped, pressing her right hand to the catch in her side.

"Good grief, Cath!" Fin pulled her inside, sat her down and fetched some water. "Drink this." He wrapped her hand around a glass and rocked back on his heels.

"Thank you," Cathy said after finishing the water and giving the glass back to him. She closed her eyes and concentrated on breathing. When she could without thinking about it, she opened them.

Fin was still on his knees in front of her. She tried not to think about how he had felt between her knees the night before, but it was impossible. He had on the black cable-knit sweater he'd worn the first time she'd seen him. A half inch or so of Houdini's scratches showed above the V neck and his jaw looked blue with a night's growth of beard.

"Did you run all the way here?"

"I tried." Cathy smiled ruefully. "Suffice it to say Florence Griffith Joyner has nothing to fear from me."

He didn't smile back. "Why didn't you drive?"

"Because Mellody parked the Mayflower behind my car and I was in no mood to ask her to move it. I was in a mood to back into it, but that would've totaled the MG and I would have ended up walking anyway, so I just eliminated the middle step."

"What's happened?"

She told him as rapidly as she could, taking a quick look around his house while she unfolded Patsy's scheme. It was all glass and wood and stone, with a wall-size fireplace and burnt-sienna carpet throughout. The furniture was simple: a sectional by the fireplace, an oak table where she sat, some chairs clustered here and there.

"Incredible," Fin uttered when she'd finished, and ran a hand through his rumpled hair as if he had suddenly remembered he hadn't combed it and was doing the best he could with his fingers. "How did Cat take it?"

"She crumpled like a paper cup. Then she went to bed."

Fin's hand froze. "You're kidding."

Cathy shook her head. "I put Houdini in with her, as much to protect him from Patsy and Mellody as to protect Grandma, but she was crying so hard I don't think she heard me. I told Had to keep an eye on the cottage and left Helmut sitting guard in his morris chair at the foot of the stairs with orders to snarl first and ask questions later."

"They wouldn't hurt the cat," Fin said, but it was more a threat than a question.

"I doubt it, but I didn't want to push Houdini's luck. Since booting him out of the house didn't work, who knows what they'll try next. Lock him in the trunk of the car?"

"Did you call your father?"

"No. I came straight here."

"Why?" Fin spread his hands on his thighs and looked at her, neither smiling nor frowning.

"Because Grandma needs help now, not when he deigns to finish the third act. Much as I'd like to, I can't throw Patsy out and I don't think Grandma will. She's too—shattered. But Patsy and Mellody have got to go so she can pull herself together and we can figure a way out of this."

"We who?" he asked curtly.

"Grandma and I, maybe Noel if I can find him. Although I'd like to throttle him, since he's the one who told Patsy all the nutty stuff Evan and Claude and the others were saying."

"Well," Fin said, more to himself than to Cathy, "isn't that interesting."

"And you, I hope." His gaze had drifted away from her, but swung back so suddenly she caught her breath. "Fin, please. She needs everyone who loves her to get her through this. Even if it never goes any further it's going to be ugly. But if it actually ends up in court—"

"You think Patsy has a case?"

"I don't know, I'm not a lawyer, but I'm scared. I know I scare easy, but I've never seen Grandma just fold up like somebody let the air out of her. I can't stand it. I—" Her throat was so tight she couldn't swallow. It made her voice crack and her eyes fill, but she plowed on. "I'll do anything. I'll stay out of your face. I won't talk to you, look at you—"

"The hell you will," he interrupted, grasping her shoulders and drawing her out of the chair as he got to his feet. "You'll not only stay in my face, you'll stay in my bed."

"No, no, you don't have to—"

"Yes, I do. Right now before I explode."

Swooping her up in his arms, Fin carried her into his bedroom. There were socks and dishes on the floor, movie posters framed on the walls and wrinkled blue sheets on an unmade king-size bed. The mattress swayed as he put her down in the middle of it and leaned over her.

"My hands are muddy," Cathy said. "I should wash them."

"Not for me." Fin smiled and laced the fingers of his right hand through her left. "Should I shave?"

"Not for me." Cathy slipped her right arm around his neck and drew him closer.

"Oh, I love a wanton woman." He chuckled and bent his head to kiss her, gently, mindful of his whiskers, then grinned at her. "I thought we were never going to end up like this, y'know. Side by side in a prone position."

"I didn't, either, and I'm so sorry—"

"Shh." He kissed her lightly. "So far we've spent most of our time shouting at each other, apologizing for shouting and then shouting some more. I've had enough."

"Me, too. More than enough."

"Sure you don't want me to shave?"

"Positive." Cathy slipped her hand free of his and wrapped both her arms around his neck. "I'm afraid to let you get up for fear we'll start shouting again."

"That's not an idle fear," Fin said with a laugh. He tried to pull away, but Cathy held him fast. "You've got to let me up for just a second," he told her. "There's a little foil packet in the drawer we're going to need and I'd just as soon fetch it now, love."

"You don't have to on my account."

"You're already protected?"

"No." Cathy tightened her arms around his neck. "But I figure if all else fails, you'll have to marry me for the sake of the children."

"Whose children?"

"Ours."

"You sure, Cath?" Fin braced himself on his hands and looked at her soberly. "This isn't the kind of thing you want to joke about with a good Irish Catholic boy."

"I'm sure," Cathy replied firmly. "I'm not getting any younger and neither is Grandma."

"God, I love you." Fin kissed her hard and quick, then reared back on his knees and peeled off his sweater. Static electricity crackled against Cathy's left index finger as she kneaded her nails through his chest hair.

Fin caught her wrist and drew her hand to his left nipple. With her fingernail Cathy teased it erect. He made a low noise in his throat and closed his eyes, capturing her fingers to nibble them and kiss her palm. The rub of his whiskers against her skin made her shiver. So did the slow, seductive slide of his right hand beneath her sweater.

"You're shaking," Fin murmured, spreading his fingers on her quivering rib cage.

"It's—been a long time," Cathy admitted shyly.

"For me, too." He smiled and so did she, raising her arms so he could rid her of the mud-spattered red sweater.

He tossed it aside, then stretched out beside her and tugged her bra straps off her shoulders to kiss the hollows of her collarbone and throat. Cathy moaned, the softness of his mouth and the friction of his beard leaving a fiery pink trail on her skin.

"Still want me to kiss you everywhere?" Fin asked, raising his head to look at her.

"Yes," Cathy whispered, taking his face in her hands and drawing his lips over hers.

He tasted like coffee and faintly of tobacco. The scrape of his whiskers against the corners of her mouth sent her head spinning. During the kiss, Fin somehow managed to free her of her bra and peel both of them out of their jeans and underwear. When she opened her eyes they were both nude and trembling.

"Oh, Fin," she murmured, drawing one finger across his bottom lip.

He sucked at her fingertip, ran his tongue around it, then traced the outline of her mouth and bent his head to ever so lightly rub his whiskered chin over her breasts. Her nipples sprang erect. Cathy held her breath, and his head between her hands, while he suckled them tenderly, blew a barely there breath over each and rubbed again with his whiskers. When his fingers slipped between her legs she opened for him and moaned. So did Fin, his fingers stroking her as he kissed his way down her stomach to taste her, tease her and cherish her.

Cathy clung to his shoulders. When he looked up at her, his face was flushed, his hair tousled and his breathing rapid. Spreading her palms, she slid them down his back as he stretched up to kiss her, reveling in the wondrous contrasts of his body: warm velvety skin and hard, hairy muscle.

"I don't think I can wait anymore," he whispered shakily, moving on top of her and spreading her legs with his.

"That makes two of us," Cathy murmured, slipping her arms around his neck as he braced himself over her with his elbows above her shoulders.

"Kiss me," he breathed against her lips.

When their opened mouths touched, he wove his fingers into her hair and thrust himself inside her. When he dragged his mouth away from hers and clung to her, his fingers quivered in her hair.

"Oh, Cath . . . Oh, God, you feel so good." He groaned raggedly, withdrawing slowly, then surging into her again. "Good, hell. You feel like heaven. Hot, velvet heaven."

Cathy was beyond speech. When Fin raised his head to kiss her again, her lashes were wet. He stopped moving and smoothed a hand across her forehead.

"Am I hurting you?"

"Oh, no," Cathy breathed, her voice and her smile quavering. "It's just—I've never been anyone's heaven."

"You won't be ever again. Anyone else's, I mean," Fin murmured against her lips, "'cause you're mine now."

And he proved it, with slow, languid thrusts that rocked Cathy's hips beneath him. Her breath caught in her throat when she wrapped her legs around him. The size and full- ness of him, the ageless, erotic thrill of having him so deeply inside her brought tears of sheer joy to her eyes. Holding his face in her hands, she kissed him, traced his lips with her tongue and arched her hips to meet him.

Fin groaned, pushed himself up on his hands and drove hard against her. With her legs Cathy clung to him, rev- eling in his fierce thrusts, the delicious friction spiraling between them. They peaked in the same shuddering in- stant, breathless and twined ecstatically together.

"Oh, Cath," Fin rumbled, sated and languid. "Oh, my love . . . my darling . . . my angel." Then he sprang up on his elbows and started singing, his voice raspy with pas- sion. "Heaven, I'm in heaven . . ."

Cathy made a face and laughed.

"Do that again," Fin begged.

"Do what?"

"Laugh."

"You are a lewd, lascivious character, McGraw."

"I know." He grinned at her. "Don't you love it?"

"Yes," Cathy confessed and kissed him.

"God, I feel better. How 'bout you?"

"Fifty-fifty," she teased, then giggled as he gnawed her ear and his beard scraped the side of her jaw.

"You're going to be head-to-toe whisker burn," he said, pushing up on his elbows again.

"Nah." Cathy wrinkled her nose at him. "Most of it my underwear will cover."

"Much as I want to, we can't spend the day in bed." He kissed her gently. "We've got a lot to do."

"Such as?"

"Would you like a shower before I tell you?"

"I'd love a shower."

"Would you love a shower with me in it?"

"Can we? I mean, without—"

"Hell, no, we can't."

And they didn't.

"Oh, my." Cathy sighed dazedly afterward as Fin wrapped her in a giant-size towel and dried her off. "I never knew you could do things like that with soap on a rope."

He chuckled and tucked the ends of the navy-blue towel beneath her chin. "I'll bring your clothes."

He did and shut the door to give her a few minutes privacy. When Cathy came out into the bedroom, Fin was dressed in a short and moldering Roman toga, a moth-eaten purple cloak, leather sandals that laced up his calves and a centurion's bristled helmet.

"What hairy knees you have, Grandma," she said haltingly.

"Ah. As brave as she is wanton," he replied admiringly. "This costume has struck terror in the hearts of virgins on four continents."

"Costume!" Cathy's eyes flew to a movie poster on a nearby wall advertising the *Creature from the Roman Baths*. The letters dripped like melted flesh over a backdrop of Roman ruins, and in the foreground— "My God, that's you! You're the Creature!"

Fin nodded grimly. "The one and only."

"Oh, darling, you terrified me!" Cathy threw her arms around his neck and laughed.

"How about the sequel?" Fin asked, sliding his hands around her waist. "Did I scare you in the sequel?"

"Senseless." She kissed him, then plucked the draped front of his toga and cocked a dubious eyebrow. "Is this why you fed me that line about the security system and nobody living here?"

"It is. The place is chock-full of Creature trivia. The hand Dr. Frobisher cuts off when I grabbed his assistant, Sylvia, the image of my beloved Flavia is a paperweight on my desk. My sword I use for a poker—"

"Oh, this is hilarious!" Cathy laughed even harder. "I've fallen in love with a monster!"

"No, Cath, Garrett is a monster. I am a Creature," he corrected her, then cupped her face tenderly in one hand. "Do you love me, really?"

"Oh, yes," Cathy murmured, "I love you really."

"All I have is this moldy old toga. I'll probably never have reviews of my stunning West End debut as Hamlet."

"Do you want a stunning West End debut?"

"Not anymore." Fin laced his fingers comfortably together behind her. "I thought I did to make up for the Creature, till it dawned on me I'd earned more doing those two campy little films than most people make in a lifetime. Made it a lot easier to turn my back on my art."

Cathy groaned and let her forehead thud against his chest. The horror film classics, the *Creature* and its sequel, had earned millions. "And I thought you were after Grandma's money," she mumbled into Fin's toga.

"That's my fault." He lifted her chin and smiled. "I wanted to make a good impression. I didn't want to risk you turning up your nose at ol' Claudius."

"I love ol' Claudius. I thought he was the sexiest thousand-year-old dead Roman centurion I'd ever seen." Cathy kissed his chin and added wickedly, "Until he started to decompose."

Fin laughed good-naturedly and hugged her. "Speaking of decomposing, want to kill two birds with one stone?"

"Which two?"

"Piranha Woman and Barracuda Girl and the lawsuit."

"How?"

"Convince them Cat's House really is haunted."

"It'll never work. You look too much like Granddad."

"I don't mean your granddad." Fin kissed her between the eyes, pried off his helmet, tossed it aside and rubbed the red mark it had left on his nose. "I mean Captain Croft."

"Oh." Cathy shivered with excitement. "I like it."

Fin unlaced his sandals, kicked them off and unfastened the brooch on his shoulder. The toga fell around his ankles, and Cathy's mouth went dry at the sight of his naked body. "Who better to raise him from the grave than a bloke who's made a bloody fortune playing a creepy old dead thing?"

"What'll we do with Houdini?"

"I'll bring him here, then nip over to the Rosebriar. The sound tech is a friend of mine." Fin pulled on his jeans, and Cathy sighed wistfully as he zipped his fly. "He's got tons of spook effects on tape."

"How about a costume? I suppose wardrobe has one."

"It just so happens," Fin said, as he tugged on a green sweater, "we're opening with the *Pirates of Penzance*."

"Perfect!" Cathy grinned and kissed him.

While he finished dressing, she put on her shoes and left the bedroom. She found the Creature's alarmingly lifelike hand on a rolltop desk near the fireplace, lying on top of a rewrite of her first chapter. Gingerly poking the hand aside, she sank into a chair and started reading Fin's large, flourishing script.

"That's not very accurate," he said behind her. "I did it from memory."

Cathy put the pad down and smiled at him over her shoulder. "It's wonderful." Fin made a mocking face at her. "It is," she insisted, rising to slip her arms around him. "Grandma fired me, you know."

"I shouldn't worry." He wrapped his arms around her waist and smiled. "She'll rehire you."

"I think she should hire you."

"I think she should hire both of us."

"A collaboration, it has possibilities . . ."

"But I must warn you—I do my best work in bed."

"What a coincidence—so do I."

"Great. We'll start tonight."

He took her hand and led her outside to his Jeep. Once they were on the way, Cathy said with a hint of excitement in her voice, "The more I think about this, the more I think it'll work."

"It'll work. But we need a stage hand."

"What about me?"

"You've got a speaking part."

"What are my lines?"

"'What moan Aunt Patsy?' 'What shriek?' 'What chain rattling?'"

"Oh, what fun!" Cathy chortled gleefully. "Maybe Noel will show up. He told Mother he'd get back here ASAP."

"I suppose he's better than nothing."

"You don't like him, do you?"

"I don't trust him." Fin frowned at her. "Those noises we heard the other night started after Cat decided to write her memoirs and the chaps your father hired started showing up. And one of them blabbed to the *Tattler*."

"It wasn't Noel," Cathy replied emphatically. "I've known him all my life. He's my father's best friend."

"I'm not pointing the finger at him necessarily." Fin let go of the gearshift and threaded his fingers through hers. "I just don't trust any of that bunch."

"You think there's something rotten on the Vineyard?"

"I do. I think somebody staged those noises and spread the ghost stories to keep people away from Cat's House."

"For heaven's sake, why?"

"Cat and I took a side trip to the Whaling Museum in New Bedford on our shopping spree the other day." Fin flicked her a grin. "Did you know Ezekiel Croft never caught a single whale in twenty years at sea?"

"But he died a wealthy old salt, darling. If he never caught a whale how did he amass his fortune?"

"Try this." Fin grinned even wider and let go of her hand to shift gears. "What if he was a pirate?"

"That would explain why Rachel dumped him, why he scuttled the ship and—" Cathy caught her breath and stared wide-eyed at him. "The earring! Grandma said she'd never seen anything like it. Where did you find it?"

"I took it away from Houdini, which means Captain Croft hid at least some of his booty in the house. And I think somebody's looking for it."

"There's something else. Captain Croft's sea chests and his maps have been rifled. Whoever did it took the time to dust off the trunks, but left the charts in a mess."

"Sounds like he, or she, was in a tearing hurry."

"D'you suppose that's what Aunt Patsy's looking for?"

"Could be. Somebody is."

"If Captain Croft did stash his booty in the house—and I suppose the earring proves that—I wonder where it is? The attic, the basement, the old root cellar . . ."

"Cat and I looked all those places and found nothing."

"So that's what Grandma was doing in the attic. And what you were doing outside. What were you looking for?"

"A false wall, an underground cache—"

"Did you, by any chance," Cathy interrupted slyly, "hope to catch Noel up to no good?"

"You're quick." Fin chuckled. "I didn't, though."

"I'm sorry I thought you were a jewel thief."

"Not to worry. I'm sure you'll find a way to make it up to me." Fin cupped his hand around her knee and grinned.

When they came through the front door a few minutes later, Helmut was still in his morris chair by the stairs.

"All quiet," he said. "Had says Patsy's been on the phone nonstop."

"To her lawyer, no doubt. Thanks, Helmut."

He grunted, rose, picked up his chair and retreated to the kitchen. Cathy and Fin went upstairs hand in hand.

Cat was on her bed with Houdini sound asleep and purring in her lap. When Fin came through the door behind Cathy, she lifted the kitten gently aside and rose on her knees to embrace him, her puffy eyes filling with fresh tears. He put his arms around her and laid his chin on her head.

Cathy smiled and hooked her elbow around the bedpost. When Cat lifted her head from Fin's chest and cast her a questioning look, she winked. Cat grinned and sat back happily on her heels.

"Okay, here's the plan." Fin sat down on the edge of the bed, smudged a tear off her chin and told her.

"It's brilliant. I, of course, will direct."

"You will keep snug in your bed in case Piranha Woman crawls under the covers with Mummy when the fun starts."

"God forbid." Cat shuddered. "I see a subtle first scene, don't you? A slow building of tension. Perhaps—"

"We haven't time for a haunting in three acts," Fin interrupted. "We hit her with everything and get her the hell out of here tonight before she has time to sweep the place again and find another flimsy piece of evidence she thinks will prove you've gone around the bend."

"Granddad's humidor!" Cathy gasped and went flying down to the library.

It was still on the corner of the desk where Noel had put it the day before. So was the white meerschaum in the rack beside the lamp. The bowl was cold and empty. How could an empty pipe smoke? Had somebody dumped the ashes? Cathy picked it up and sniffed. It still smelled stale. Weird. Frowning, she put it back, and started as the doorbell rang.

It was Noel. His tan Mercedes was parked in the driveway behind Fin's Jeep.

"I'm sorry, Cathy," he said earnestly as she opened the door. "Believe me, if I'd known Patsy would pull something like this I would never have called her."

"I know that, Noel. Still, you deserve horsewhipping."

"I know that, too." He winced. "Is there anything I can do to make up for it?"

Cathy smiled. "It just so happens there is."

18

By TWO O'CLOCK Houdini was safely stashed at Fin's house and the Green Rooms were ready for Patsy and Mellody. The linens were fresh, the furniture dusted and a speaker ingeniously modified from a car stereo was hidden in the bathroom light fixture. The weather even lent a hand by turning cloudy and blustery.

"Won't be n'rain," Had pronounced once he'd finished drilling the hole in the ceiling, through which he'd fed the wires that connected the speaker to the reel-to-reel recorder also on loan from the Rosebriar and set up in the attic mishmash room. "Just a blow."

While Noel and Fin tested the system, Cathy went to the kitchen. Helmut handed her a knife, two yellow onions and thumbed her toward the cutting board.

"Tear ducts, don't fail me now." Cathy drew a deep breath and started chopping.

Within half an onion her eyes were streaming; an onion and a half later she looked as if she'd been crying for hours. After washing her hands, she grabbed a fistful of tissues and made a beeline for the guest cottage.

When Patsy opened the door, Cathy blubbered that Houdini had run out of the house behind her that morning, and please, oh, please, if she or Mellody saw him would they tell her. Of course, Patsy gushed, and Cathy sniffled back to the house.

Noel set the stopwatch on his wrist chronometer; three minutes and forty-seven seconds later, Patsy and Mellody came trooping through the Dutch door.

"Since the cat has moved on, we are moving in," Patsy told her mother. "I trust you have no objection."

"Why, heavens no, dear." Cat made a bow of her lips and fluttered her lashes.

The belligerent jut of Patsy's chin said she'd expected a fight, not instant capitulation. It threw her for a few seconds, then she announced they'd take the Green Rooms, and swept Mellody up the stairs.

In their wake, Fin gave Cat a high five and kissed Cathy. "You'll help me into my costume later, won't you?"

"I'd rather help you out of it," she murmured, her lips tingling from the sandpaper brush of his whiskered chin.

He'd decided not to shave to lend Captain Croft a fiercer countenance, which was fine with Cathy, who at last understood the appeal of the stubbled look.

When they came downstairs, Patsy parked herself in the library to discuss Cat's memoirs, and Mellody stalked Fin, waiting for an opportunity to trip him and beat him to the floor. By five o'clock when everyone went up to change for dinner, Cathy had decided to forego the Barbie doll and use the nails directly on Mellody.

"Why did I have children?" Cat muttered to her as they climbed the stairs. "Why didn't I sign to make a movie in Outer Mongolia instead?"

Cathy showered, and after running Cat's bath, went through the sitting room to her bedroom. Fin was waiting in her bed.

"Lock that," he said huskily, and threw back the sheet.

Cathy did, ripping off her terry-cloth robe as she fell on top of him. They kissed hungrily, then clung together.

"How did you escape Mellody?"

"I told her to wait for me in my room."

"Oh, you clever man."

"Where there's a will there's a way."

Fin trailed kisses from her mouth to her breasts, gently brushing his whiskers across her nipples.

"Oh, darling—" Cathy moaned "—promise me you'll throw your razor away."

He chuckled and rolled her onto her back, his left hand splayed and sliding down her stomach.

"We don't have time for this."

"We won't have time later."

"You're right. Kiss me, you fool."

He did, not everywhere, but close. Their joining was not as languid as their first in Fin's water bed, nor as quick as their second in the shower, but every bit as urgent.

"Ain't love grand?" Fin murmured in her ear, listening to the fierce gusts outside the bedroom window, which almost matched the storm that had raged within. "It's almost show time."

"Are you nervous?"

"Nope. Scaring the hell outta people is what I do best."

"Not by a long shot, darling."

He grinned and kissed her, then rolled to his feet and began to dress. Cathy was all thumbs trying to button the silk camp shirt she'd chosen to wear with pink slacks. She stood at the mirror to do it, still fouled it up and started over.

"Let me." Fin came up behind her, slid his hands under her arms and quickly did up the buttons. "Stage fright?"

Cathy nodded. He slipped his arms around her waist and smiled at her in the mirror. He looked incredibly handsome with his finger-combed hair falling over his forehead. It struck Cathy then that she couldn't remember the last time she'd thought how much he looked like her grandfather.

"You're wearing Granddad's suspenders again."

"I've never fancied braces much," he admitted, "but I like these. Thought I'd wear them for luck."

He quickly kissed her temple, and they went through the sitting room to collect Cat for dinner.

The first course was French onion soup. "Waste not want not," Helmut muttered in Cathy's ear as he put hers down in front of her. The second was fillet of sole. When everyone was served, Fin nodded to Cat, and the play began.

"Darling girl, did you tidy up Captain Croft's chests?"

"Yes. They're all shipshape and ready to go."

"Go where?" Patsy asked. "What are you giving away now, Mother?"

"Nothing of any monetary value, Patricia." Cat shot her a sharp look. "I'm donating Captain Croft's sea charts to the Whaling Museum in New Bedford."

"Oh, well. I suppose that's all right."

"They don't get the house until I'm dead."

"What?" Patsy nearly dropped her fork. "You can't give this house away! It's worth a fortune!"

"Speaking of fortunes." Cat jumped on the cue. "You'll never guess why the museum is interested in the captain's things."

"I give up," Patsy replied between clenched teeth.

"The curator believes he may have been a pirate and his treasure is hidden in the house!"

Patsy's fork hit the table. Mellody's eyes gleamed at Fin. Noel choked.

"Bone—" he gasped, clapping his napkin over his mouth and ducking into the kitchen.

"How much treasure?" Patsy asked.

"Who knows? But we do have a hint." Cat produced the emerald-and-diamond earring from her pocket and held it up to the glow of the candles burning on the table. "Houdini found this little bauble."

Patsy reached for it, but Cat snatched it away. "Little bauble..." she murmured, her sentence trailing off and her eyes turning misty.

She was definitely interested, but Cathy was willing to bet this was the first she'd heard of pirate treasure.

"I've just had the most wonderful idea," Patsy said. "Let's have a treasure hunt tomorrow."

"Wonderful!" Cat agreed enthusiastically. "Wouldn't it be lovely if I could turn Captain Croft's booty over to the museum along with his sea chests?"

"You'll do no such thing!" Patsy declared.

"But of course I will," Cat replied matter-of-factly. "This is my house, and I can do what I damn well please."

"For God's sake, Mother! It could be worth millions!"

"So am I, dear. I don't need the money."

"But I do!" Patsy bit her lip, but too late.

"And so," Cat said sadly, "the truth at last."

"You have no right," Patsy said, her voice shaking, "to hand my legacy over to strangers."

"It's not your legacy," Cat retorted. "It's Captain Croft's, and I can't think of a more ironically fitting place to see it end up than the Whaling Museum."

"At least she isn't giving it to her darling girl," Mellody chimed in petulantly.

"Oh, shut up!" Patsy shrilled at her, then glared at Cat. "You're insane, Mother!"

"Prove it," Cat challenged with a serene smile.

"I intend to!" She threw her napkin on the table. "Come along, Mellie."

They stormed up the stairs to the Green Rooms, the slam of the door behind them echoing along the gallery. Cat set her jaw and quaffed her wine. Noel edged back into the dining room, a sympathetic half smile on his face.

"I'm sorry, Grandma," Cathy said quietly.

"It could be worse." Cat sniffed and put down her goblet. "She could be my only child."

"I doubt they'll be down again this evening," Fin said.

"Let us pray." Cat sniffed again and rose. "Now let's have a run-through in the library."

They checked places and props, discussed possible scenarios and kicked around lines until ten o'clock when the lights went out in the Green Rooms, and Fin got to his feet.

"The tape will roll at ten-thirty sharp," he told Cathy and Cat. To Noel he added, "Give me a few minutes to get into my costume. Then come on up."

"Will do."

Fin hugged Cat and kissed Cathy. "Make sure Cat gets to bed all right," he whispered in her ear.

"Don't you want help with your costume?"

"Penney can lend a hand if I need it. Love you." He kissed her again quickly and slipped up the stairs.

"Love you, too," Cathy murmured, then turned to see her grandmother regarding the library thoughtfully.

"You know, darling, I think we should lock the doors," she said suddenly and moved past her to close them.

"They've been open for days," Noel reminded her.

"Yes, I know. But under the circumstances—"

A mournful yowl from the front porch interrupted her.

"Houdini!" Cathy hurried into the foyer with Cat and Noel behind her, flipped on the light, undid the locks and opened the door. "You little sneak! How did you get out of Fin's house?"

The kitten yowled again, less stridently, and rubbed against the screen door. The howling wind had flattened his ears and sleeked his black fur against his body.

"You can't leave him outside," Noel said.

"We can't bring him in the house, either," Cat replied.

"How about if we put him in the basement?" Cathy suggested.

They did, but he only howled louder.

"Let him up," Cat said, "before he wakes the dead."

"Please, Grandma."

"Sorry, darling."

When she opened the door, Houdini slipped past it and through Cathy's fingers as she bent to pick him up.

"Damn it, Houdini, come here!" She cursed, chasing him around the corner into Helmut's bedroom.

"Hey, li'l buddy," Helmut rumbled as the kitten arched against his ankles, then slid past him to yowl and rub the back wall beneath the wainscoting.

Li'l buddy? Openmouthed, Cathy watched Helmut unfold his bulk from the morris chair, bend over and gently scoop the kitten up in one hand.

"Put 'im in the ol' lady's room, y'might need him," he said, handing Houdini to her. "Take a can a salmon and he'll be happy as a clam."

"Better be quick about it," Noel urged, tapping the face of his watch. "We should all be on our marks."

"Off with you, then." Cat gave him a push. "We'll be along in a moment."

Noel went, and Cathy tucked Houdini securely into the curve of her arms.

"Staying up to watch the fun, Helmut?"

"Sorta. Me an' Had are the outside patrol."

He winked; Cathy winked back and took Houdini and her grandmother upstairs. "Clever old Helmut," she said once they were in Cat's room. "If all else fails, we can sic Houdini on her."

"Too bad," Cat muttered, "he isn't a panther."

Since both the bedroom doors were shut, Cathy let Houdini roam while she helped Cat get ready for bed. Once her grandmother was tucked into the four-poster, Cathy leaned over her, and Cat cupped her face in both hands.

"Break a leg, darling girl."

"You, too, Grandma. I'll leave the bathroom light on."

They exchanged a smacking kiss, and Cathy hurried into her bedroom. She was shaking again, but with excitement now, as she hastily stripped off her clothes and threw on pajamas and a kimono. She mussed up her hair with her fingers, licked her index fingers and laid them against her eyelashes to smear her mascara, then sat down on the side of the bed she and Fin had rumpled, and pressed her hands together between her knees.

"C'mon, darling," she murmured into the darkness. "Scare the bejesus out of 'em."

The trees banged nonstop against the eaves, the moon dipped in and out of the clouds racing away beneath it. A great night for a haunting, Cathy thought. She jumped at a solid thump above her and then again at another thump, a crash and a muffled outcry.

"'Atta boy, guys." She grinned, then shivered with anticipation at the creak of slow, furtive footsteps descending the steps.

Cathy held herself ready on the edge of the bed, listening and glancing at the clock radio she'd brought down from the attic. Ten forty-seven. The tape had been running for seventeen minutes. Surely it had wakened Patsy and Mellody by now. Any minute now, any second—

Houdini yowled on the gallery.

"Oh, hell!" Cathy leaped to her feet, flung open her door and almost collided with Cat, who was trying to grab Houdini. The great escape artist slithered between Cathy's ankles, rounded the gallery and made for the Green Rooms.

"Head him off!" Cat shoved Cathy one way as she went the other.

But Houdini was already skimming down the last flight of stairs, his coat gleaming in the broken moonlight as he cut toward the kitchen, and Cathy and Cat came nose to nose on the landing.

"Why did you let him out of your room?"

"Why did you open my door?"

"I didn't!"

"Somebody did!" Cat grabbed Cathy's wrist and nodded at the thin line of light showing beneath Patsy's bedroom door. "There's your cue, darling girl! *Go!* I'll get the cat."

Cathy went up the stairs and along the gallery into Cat's room to shut and lock the door behind her, then through the sitting room to fling herself, heart thumping, on the bed. This haunting's off to a roaring start, she thought, just as a throat-tearing shriek came from the Green Rooms.

"Here we go," she said, reaching for the lamp as she rolled to her feet. She flipped the switch but nothing happened. "Oh, nice touch, fellas." Cathy grinned and hurried to open the door.

Her aunt and cousin were already on the gallery, Mellody hunched and shivering in her mother's arms. "There, baby, there," Patsy murmured, her voice quavering.

Cathy snickered evilly to herself as she shuffled toward them. "Whas th' matter?" she asked around a feigned, jaw-stretching yawn.

"Cathy?" her aunt queried shrilly.

"Did one of you guys scream or was I dreaming?"

"It was Mellie," Patsy said. "I thought she was dreaming, but then I heard it, too, and the lights went out and—"

Ker-whack! The attic door burst open like a thunderclap. Mellody screamed, and Patsy's mouth fell open. So did Cathy's as she spun around and saw a flickering cloud of light spilling down the stairs. Wow, she thought wondrously.

"Oh, my God!" Patsy squeaked. "What is it?"

Cathy turned again to ask sleepily, "What's what, Aunt Patsy?"

Patsy didn't answer except for a strangled cry and started backing slowly toward the stairs with Mellody.

"Mama, what is it?" Mellody asked in a tiny, shaky voice.

Patsy clapped a hand over her eyes. "Don't look, baby."

If her aunt hadn't so richly deserved this for breaking Cat's heart and Mellody for drop-kicking Houdini off the veranda, Cathy might have felt sorry for them. A small part of her—well, okay, a teensy-weensy part—wanted to admit it was all a hoax. Instead she hissed, "Scaredy-cats," at them under her breath, and turned back to the attic.

Goose bumps raced through her body at the swirling apparition taking shape in the midst of the flickering cloud. The special effects were better than ol' Claudius rising in a bloody mist from the sunken ruins of the bath where Flavia's brother had murdered him.

Grinning, Cathy watched the apparition separate from the mist and glide out onto the gallery. On the landing, mouth agape, Patsy was frozen with horror by the sight floating toward her.

Prying herself loose from her mother's fingers, Mellody looked up and screamed. Then she grabbed Patsy's wrist and jerked her down the stairs.

"Run little knickerbockers!" Cathy cried gleefully. "Run, run, run!"

On the landing, Fin paused and beckoned to Cathy, his raised arm spiraling jeweled light. How was he doing that? He beckoned her again, then drifted away after Patsy and Mellody. Cathy raced after him down the steps, past the French doors in the dining room and into the kitchen.

Once through the doorway, Fin spurted ahead of her into the back hall. How was he making it look as if his feet weren't touching the floor? What a performance! What grace, what fluidity of motion! Her grandmother had never seen Fin at his best.

"Fin, wait!" Cathy called.

He did, but only for a fraction of a heartbeat, until she came around the cabinets behind him. He raised his hand to her, made a midair pirouette and vanished out the open Dutch door, just as Houdini came tearing through it and shot into Helmut's bedroom.

What was the kitten doing outside? Where was Cat? Cathy stepped out onto the patio, the wind snapping the hem of her kimono as she took a quick look around. There was no sign of her grandmother or Fin—or of Helmut, Had or Noel.

Cathy ducked inside, hit the wall switch but nothing happened. She opened the kitchen junk drawer, fumbled for the flashlight, found it and followed Houdini into Helmut's bedroom. He was rubbing the wall again and yowled mournfully as Cathy switched on the flashlight. His tail bristled. His gold eyes were huge.

"C'mere, Houdini." Cathy reached for him, but he leaped away and dived under Helmut's bed. "C'mon,

Houdini!" She went down on her knees, stuck her head and the flashlight under the bed and saw him cowering against the far wall. "Come out of there, you little pill."

He blinked at her and backed farther into the corner. Cathy couldn't reach him; instead she rose, pulled the bed out and scrambled across it on all fours. Houdini bolted as she reached for him, but so did Cathy, launching herself toward the foot and making a diving grab for him that missed and sent her smacking headfirst into the wall.

She saw stars and she saw the wall swing inward with a groaning creak. Stunned, Cathy thought she'd managed another concussion until Houdini slithered past the opening. When the tip of his tail disappeared, she scrambled off the bed, gave the wall a push and shone the flashlight down a flight of narrow, timeworn steps.

19

IT TOOK CATHY five seconds to realize what she'd found, and another twenty or so to drag Helmut's morris chair across the floor to hold the panel open. Then she gripped the flashlight tight in her right hand and picked her way carefully down the steps. They were cut out of stone, very narrow, and gleamed with damp. There was no banister, so she pressed her left palm against the cold stone wall to steady her descent.

Halfway down she dropped gingerly to her heels with her back against the wall and made a slow sweep with the flashlight of a small room with a rough stone floor and walls and several thick wooden beams supporting the low ceiling. Cat was tied to one of them near the center.

"Grandma!" Cathy cried.

Cat raised her chin and blinked in the glare of the flashlight. She was gagged, with the belt of her pink chenille robe, and Cathy all but broke her neck slipping and falling the rest of the way down the steps to get to her.

Laying the flashlight aside, she tugged the gag from Cat's mouth. Cat drew a shaky but deep breath and smiled tremulously as Cathy cupped her face in her hands. She was shivering and her skin felt icy.

"Are you all right, Grandma?"

"I will be as soon as you untie me," she said, her voice quavering. "Hurry, darling, my bursitis is killing me."

"Who did this?" Cathy scrambled behind her to untie the rest of the pink chenille belt.

"Noel. God help him."

"He had better if I get my hands on him." The knot came undone; Cathy grasped her grandmother's elbows, lifted her to her feet and embraced her.

Cat was trembling violently now, from reaction as much as the cold. Cathy held her closer, chafed her palms up and down her spine to warm her. Through the backwash of the flashlight beam bouncing off the far wall she saw Houdini sniff around three small wooden chests.

"I don't have to ask why. I think I'm looking at why."

"The chests? He made off with one." Cat pressed her cheek briefly to Cathy's shoulder, then turned out of her arms. "The one I opened. It was full of jewelry. Fabulous stuff."

"How did you find the steps, Grandma?"

"This little bugger," she said, stroking Houdini's back as he jumped atop one of the chests and began to purr. "I chased him down to Helmut's room, tripped over the morris chair in the dark and hit the wall with my shoulder, hard enough apparently to trip the catch and aggravate my bursitis. Houdini came down, I followed—"

"In the pitch-black?" Cathy blurted.

"I had my trusty lighter. I'd no more than seen the chests and opened one when Noel appeared. He let Houdini out of my bedroom, having surmised from what we said about the earring at dinner that if anyone knew where Captain Croft's cache was it was Houdini."

At the sound of his name, the kitten leaped into Cat's arms. She scratched his ears; he purred louder and rubbed his head beneath her chin.

"How d'you know all this, Grandma?"

"Can you believe the bastard told me? Actually had the *nerve* to apologize for leaving me down here to rot while he went to find the cat and drown him so no one else would find this place?"

"How did Houdini get away?"

"Went up the stairs like a shot the second he saw Noel."

Cathy sat down hard on one of the chests, gripped the splintered edge of the lid and shook. If Houdini hadn't gotten away, if she hadn't followed him into Helmut's room, if she hadn't hit her head . . .

"Surely, Grandma," she asked, looking up at Cat, "Noel meant to set you free once he'd removed the other chests?"

"*Really*, darling girl." Cat eyed her granddaughter incredulously over Houdini's ears. "You can't be that naive."

Grabbing the flashlight off the floor, Cathy stood and opened all three chests. She had to see what they held.

"Holy moley," she breathed, dazzled by the array of jewelry, silver plate, uncut stones, bars of gold and heaps of coins. "It's awesome, but it's not worth your life."

"Avarice can make even the kindest people do terrible things," Cat said quietly. "Which prompts me to ask, how went the haunting?"

"Wonderfully. Fin was incredible. Utterly terrifying."

"Really?" Cat remarked thoughtfully. "Is it possible he can act?"

"Of course he can act," Cathy replied defensively, and started to shut the chests. "Olivier may never have to watch his back for Fin McGraw, but if the role calls for gut-wrenching terror, then he's the man to call. He gave me the heebie-jeebies and I knew it was him."

As Cathy's hand closed on the lid of the last trunk, Houdini leaped into it. He dug through the gems, came up with a ruby brooch the size of a walnut in his mouth and raced up the steps with it.

"What's this?" Cathy lifted the frayed end of a scarlet ribbon Houdini had uncovered. She tugged, felt the weight of something attached to it, passed the flashlight to Cat, brushed jewels out of the way—and caught her breath. A chill shot up her back as she lifted the tied-together bundle out of the chest and held it under the beam.

"I knew it!" she crowed, giddy with delight as she read the faded script on brittle parchment. "Rachel's letters! I told you they were here someplace!"

"So you did," Cat admitted. "Well, I'll be damned."

Cathy had spent half her girlhood looking for these, and now she'd found them. But first she'd found the sabertooth. And so had Noel.

"Oh, God," she said weakly, remembering him holding it belly up in his hands, and how threatened she'd felt. "I thought it was odd Noel asked all those questions."

"About what?"

"The tiger. He wanted to know precisely where I'd found it. It's a little piece of the *Rachel Simms*. The name's burned on the tiger's belly." Cathy bit her lip and looked at her grandmother. "You suspected Noel all along, didn't you? That's why you had Daddy fire him."

"I'm sorry, darling." Cat brushed her knuckles gently across her cheek. "You're very fond of him, I know, but—"

"Don't be sorry!" Cathy hugged her fiercely, felt again how frail she was as the flashlight bumped between her shoulder blades and bit back tears. "I could have lost you because of Noel!"

"But you didn't." Cat held her at arm's length and smiled. "You *found* me, darling girl. If you hadn't, I would have been truly lost."

What if Fin hadn't gone into the kitchen? What if she hadn't followed him, and then Houdini, into Helmut's room? Cathy shivered.

"Hey, ol' lady!" Helmut shouted from the top of the stairs. "You down there?"

"Yes, Helmut!" Cat called up to him and slipped her arm through Cathy's. "My darling girl is with me!"

"Better get up here, then. The cops're comin'."

"Did you catch him, Helmut?"

He made a rude, derisive snort, and Cathy and Cat grinned at each other.

The floor lamp in Helmut's room was on and so were the kitchen lights. The Dutch door and the French doors were shut, and when Cathy followed her grandmother into the living room, Helmut was standing with his arms folded on one side of the window seat and Had was on the other with his hoe. Between them sat Noel, his left hand pressed to the small of his back. His eyes lifted hopefully toward Cathy, but when she stopped in the gap of the quarter-deck rail and looked pointedly away, he lowered his head and swept his right hand over his mouth.

"Where's Patsy?" Cat asked.

"Long gone," Helmut said. "Her an' the little man-eater lit outta here doin' sixty in reverse up the drive-way."

"Nope," Had disagreed. "Believe it was nearer seventy."

"Where's Fin?" Cathy asked.

"Beats me." Helmut shrugged indifferently.

"Had, have you seen him?"

"Nope. Seen yer granddad a while ago."

"But Fin went outside—I assumed to help you guys— once he'd chased off Aunt Patsy and Mellody." She glared at Noel. "You put the idea of the lawsuit in her head, didn't you? Once Grandma was trucked off to the nearest nursing home, you'd have had all the time in the world to find Captain Croft's treasure."

"You want me to admit it?" Noel asked heavily.

"I wouldn't admit anything," Cathy advised, "not till you talk to a lawyer. Maybe Patsy will post your bail. If she does, and you feel inclined to tell her about the trick we played on her, go right ahead. I saw her face when she saw Fin, and I doubt very seriously she'll believe you."

"I'm not going to tell her." He winced and rubbed his sacroiliac. "Could I have a chair? My back's killing me."

"Hurt himself heftin' the jewel chest," Had explained.

"If I hadn't, you wouldn't have caught me."

"Don't bet on it," Helmut snarled, taking a threatening step toward the window seat.

Noel scooted quickly away from him, then looked at Cathy. "The last time I saw McGraw he was tied and gagged in the attic. I don't know who let him out."

"I certainly didn't," Cat snorted.

Helmut shook his head.

"Nope." Had said.

Cathy felt every hair on her body stand on end, then whirled and raced up the stairs, along the gallery and up again into the attic. The lights were on and the recorder was still running. Fin was lying on the floor on his right side, his eyes closed, a red sash tied around the lower half of his face, his wrists tied behind him to his ankles with an old venetian-blind cord.

He'd been here the whole time. "Seen yer granddad a while ago," Had had said. Cathy's knees gave out and she folded up on her heels beside Fin. His eyes sprang open, leaped wider when he saw her. Cathy threw her arms around him and clung to him, trembling. She yanked the sash off his mouth and kissed him as hard as she could.

She felt his teeth behind his lips, his heart beating, smelled a faint trace of her perfume in his hair from their lovemaking. He wasn't a ghost, he was real. He was flesh and blood. He was hers and she wasn't going to lose him now that she'd found him.

"Darling, are you all right?" Cathy asked, her fingertips unsteady against his chin.

"Are you? You're pale as death and shaking like a leaf. What's happened?"

"Lots of things. But Grandma's fine, you're fine, Patsy and Mellody are gone and Helmut and Had are holding Noel for the police."

"Quick, then. Get me the hell out of this so I can go punch the bastard before they get here."

Cathy did, as quickly as she could. Fin drew her into his lap, kissed her and buried his face in the hollow of her throat. Cathy wrapped her arms around him and cradled him to her breast.

"Promise you'll kiss me till my lips bleed once a day," he murmured and raised his head.

Tracing the curve of his jaw and his nose with her still-unsteady fingertips, Cathy thought how much he looked like her grandfather and felt tears in her eyes.

"What is it?" Fin asked gently, cradling her cheek in his hand. "Why are you crying?"

"I can't tell you. I want to and I will, but I—I just can't right now." Resting her head on his shoulder, she cried until the lace-frilled front of his shirt was soaked, then sniffed and mopped clumsily at the tearstains with the sleeve of her kimono. "I don't cry very often."

"Oh, good. Neither do I." Fin wiped away the last of her tears with his thumbs, eased her out of his lap, got stiffly to his feet and helped her up.

Beneath the lace-fronted shirt, he wore over-the-knee cuffed boots and black leather pants. They hugged his thighs as the peel hugs a banana.

"Promise you'll wear those pants at our wedding," Cathy said with a crooked smile.

"You got it." Fin laughed and led her downstairs.

They turned the corner on the landing in time to see Noel being led through the foyer in handcuffs by two uniformed officers. Cat was on the window seat smoking, Houdini curled beside her. Had was gone, but Helmut stood at the fireplace. He nodded to Cathy as she and Fin came through the quarterdeck rail, then went to his room.

"I'm sorry, Grandma." Cathy sat beside her and took her hand. "I should have been here."

"No, darling, it was nothing, really. I'm to present myself tomorrow to formally press charges."

"But you aren't going to, are you?"

"To what end? There's no real harm done. Helmut and Hadley recovered the chest, and Noel has already been dealt the worst punishment he could possibly suffer."

"Meaning he didn't get away clean with ol' Zeke's treasure," Fin said.

"Precisely." Cat smiled. "How are you, dear boy?"

"Embarrassed that I let myself get sucker punched. Beyond that, well enough."

"Indeed." Cat gave his leather pants the once-over and raised a skeptical brow. "Do you mean to wear those trousers on stage?"

"I do," he said solemnly, winking at Cathy. She groaned and he laughed. "But I may be wearing them at your granddaughter's wedding first."

"Does this mean," Cat asked, turning to Cathy, "that I may actually hold my great-grandchild in my arms before I die?"

It would be damn difficult to do so after, Cathy started to say, but since she was no longer sure, she just smiled.

20

THE THREE OF THEM WENT for a walk on the beach the next morning, Cat with her umbrella between Cathy and Fin. Since they'd spent the night in each other's arms in Fin's room at the end of the hall, they didn't mind being apart for a little while.

After breakfast, Cat retired to the greenhouse and Cathy to the library. Supposedly to write, but when Fin brought her a cup of coffee she was sitting in front of a blank screen with her grandfather's white meerschaum in her hands.

He sat on the corner of the desk, laid his forearm on his knee and smiled. "I'm going to make myself scarce for a while. I really should pick up the socks in my bedroom and run the dishwasher."

"Don't do it for me," Cathy replied. "I'm a lousy house-keeper. No, that's a lie. I'm a slob."

"What a coincidence." He snapped his fingers. "So am I." He kissed her. "But I think you need some time alone with Cat."

"You are," she said gently, "a very perceptive man."

"Not to mention handsome as the devil, charming, talented—"

"Go home and pick up your socks, Fin," Cathy cut in and wrinkled her nose at him. "I'll be along in a while to help you."

"Hurry." He gave her another quick kiss and slid off the desk.

Cathy put the pipe back in the rack, shut off the computer and went out to the greenhouse. Cat was at the potting bench in her coveralls and apron, piddling with bright red and vivid salmon geraniums. Houdini lay stretched on the window ledge, sound asleep and purring.

"Hello, darling." Cat smiled. "Where's Fin?"

"He went home to pick up his socks." Cathy hied herself onto the bench, gripped the edge with both hands and took a deep breath. "Grandma, was it really him last night?"

"I don't know, darling girl, I didn't see him."

"Had said he saw him."

"Hadley is *forever* saying he sees him. And for all I know, he does."

"Haven't you? Seen him, I mean?"

"No. Not since the day he dropped dead at my feet." Cat scooped a trowel full of soil into a pot, then pursed her lips. "No. Perhaps swoon is a better word. It really was the most elegant fall I've ever seen. What innate grace he had. He and Barrymore."

"Yes, I noticed that last night," Cathy murmured.

Cat put down her trowel and looked at her. "What does it matter if it was or wasn't really him?"

"I saw him, Grandma, I know I saw him, but—"

"You can't believe it, can you?" Cat smiled and got up from the bench. "One is never truly dead, not as in doornails or mackerels. There's an essence that remains."

"Does Granddad's essence ever smoke a pipe? Is that why you keep tobacco for him?"

"Hadley says he does, but I couldn't say. I keep the tobacco for *me*, darling girl. I grieved for him for the longest time, you know, and the tobacco helped me remember all the joy we shared. Perhaps it's one of the things that drew him back."

"Dad said you used to smoke his pipes."

"Oh, that Lindsay!" Cat laughed, but a telltale flush pinked her cheeks. "What a kidder!"

"I smelled Autumn Orchard in the library, Grandma, the day I arrived. When I put you to bed, I took the key out of your pocket, and when I opened the library, Granddad's meerschaum was in his pipe rack, lit and smoking. You didn't light it, because I had the key. And how did the pipe get through a locked door?"

"What an interesting little trick. Shall I ask him how he did that?"

"You do talk to him, then?"

"Not as I talk to you, but there is an—awareness."

"You're being very vague, Grandma," Cathy said impatiently. "I'm trying to understand, but you're not helping."

"Try this." Cat peeled off her ugly gloves and took Cathy's hands in hers. "You love Fin desperately and he loves you. You're apart, but you're thinking of him and you know he's thinking of you. You *feel* it. It's very like that with Phineas and I."

"But he's dead, Grandma."

"Not to me, darling," Cat said softly. "To me he's merely somewhere else. I don't see him because I don't need to see him to know he's with me. Perhaps you saw him last night because you needed to know he's here."

The same thing had already occurred to Cathy. She felt tears in her eyes and blinked them away.

"Don't let it trouble you." Cat smoothed one hand across her forehead. "He'd be quite distraught if he knew he'd upset you."

"I swore I wasn't going to tell you this, but—he led me into the kitchen and the back hall, and then he—he waited for me, Grandma." Cathy paused to take a breath, but it didn't help; tears spilled down her cheeks. "Either for me or Houdini to make his entrance so I'd be sure to follow him and find you, I don't know—and then he raised his hand like he was waving and—and then he was gone." She threw her arms around Cat and sobbed. "And I never got to say, 'Thanks, Granddad,' or—or 'I love you, Granddad,' or—or anything."

"But he knows that." Cat held her close and stroked her hair. "Do you know why I call you darling girl?"

"N-no," she stammered.

Cat smiled and cupped Cathy's face in her hands. "Because that's what he called you. His little darling girl."

"Oh, God!" Cathy wailed, cried some more and then resolutely dragged the backs of her hands across her eyes. "I told Fin I don't cry very often. What a lie."

"Sometimes it's good for you." Cat patted her cheek and sat down again at the bench. Houdini stretched off the ledge to curl up and purr in her lap.

"I think he was here because you were in danger, Grandma."

"Quite probably. Though as strong as his presence has been the past few days I thought perhaps—" Cat checked herself, her fingers stilling as she stroked Houdini's ears. Then she shrugged and picked up her trowel. "Oh, well. It's of no matter now."

Since she'd read *We've Been Here Before*, Cathy knew precisely what she'd meant to say. "Don't even think it."

"I'm not thinking it, and I'm certainly in no hurry. We're all going to London in a few weeks—you and I and Fin, that is, he'll tell you why—and I've my great-grandchild to see before I die." Cat put down her trowel and frowned. "So why are you sitting there? I am a very old woman. Go help Fin pick up the socks."

"In a minute. There's one more thing. 'A soul abruptly parted from the body . . . tends to reincarnate . . .'"

"Oh, *that*." Cat gave a haughty, dismissive wave, yet flushed. "It's nothing. Forget it."

"I'm not leaving till you explain it."

"Oh, very well, for the sake of my great-grandchild," she grumbled. "Initially Fin was reluctant to have a go at play-writing, so when I ran across that I thought—"

"You could bamboozle him with it," Cathy cut in.

"I don't care for your choice of words," Cat retorted stiffly, "but that's the upshot of it, yes."

"Grandma." Cathy tsked and shook her head.

"Will you please go now?"

"Yes." Cathy slid off the bench and kissed her on the mouth. "I love you, Grandma."

"I love you, darling girl." Cat patted her cheek. "I'd very much like a great-granddaughter."

"I'll tell Fin."

"I already did."

Cathy wasn't surprised; she just chuckled and kissed the top of Cat's head, gave Houdini's ears a quick scratch, then went into the house for her car keys. On her way downstairs she saw Rachel's letters lying on the breakfront where she'd put them the night before. She'd take them with her, she decided, so she and Fin could read them in bed. After they'd picked up the socks.

She tucked them under her arm and turned to leave, her gaze catching on the driftwood tiger crouched between the candlesticks on the mantel. Cathy paused a moment, then went to the fireplace and picked it up, turned it over, ran one finger over *Rachel Simms* and smiled.

What was the saber-tooth anyway, beyond a physical manifestation of a little girl's dream fulfilled. Now that she had Rachel's letters and Fin, her heart's desire, there wasn't so much as a flicker in the tiger's eyes. Since she knew what the saber-tooth was now, Cathy wasn't surprised. Maybe it really had winked at her, or maybe she'd imagined it. Either way, some things were best left unexplained.

And better still, put back where they belonged.

Leaving her car keys in place of the tiger, Cathy headed for the beach. She took her time, looking for just the right spot, and picked one near a jagged outcropping of rock about halfway between Cat's House and Fin's A-frame.

"Thanks, Rachel." Cathy planted a kiss on the saber-tooth's nose, drew back her arm and threw.

It turned end over end as it fell and splashed into the surf with a plop. Cathy waited a minute to make sure it didn't wash back onto the beach, then smiled, satisfied, and turned toward Fin's house.

He'd been watching for her, because he came trotting out to the beach to sweep her up and kiss her.

"I had a feeling you'd walk," he said, slipping his arm around her waist and turning her toward the house. "What've you got there?"

"Rachel's love letters to Captain Croft. They're part of what I couldn't tell you last night." Cathy wrapped her arm around his waist and leaned her head on his shoulder. "But I think I can tell you today."

She tipped her head back to look up at him, and he kissed the bridge of her nose. "Before or after?"

"Your choice."

"Tell me now, then. Once we get to it, I plan to spend about the next eight hours in bed."

"First, tell me why we're going to London."

"Ready or not, to make a third Creature flick. The producer called yesterday morning, and to make a long story short, he made me an offer I can't refuse."

"How're they going to resurrect ol' Claudius this time? I thought Frobisher hacked him to bits in the last one."

"You haven't eaten recently, have you?"

"No."

"Regenerative tissue."

"Oh, yuk!" Cathy laughed and made a face.

"I agree, but there's a bright side."

"What's that?"

At the foot of the deck stairs, he turned her into his arms and laced his fingers together in the small of her back. "Art imitates life, right?"

Cathy clasped her hands behind him and smiled. "So I'm told."

"This time," Fin said with a grin, "I get the girl."

COMING NEXT MONTH

Harlequin Superromance®

A powerful restaurant conglomerate that draws the best and brightest to its executive ranks. Now almost eighty years old, Vanessa Hamilton, the founder of Hamilton House, must choose a successor.
Who will it be?

Matt Logan: He's always been the company man, the quintessential team player. But tragedy in his daughter's life and a passionate love affair made him make some hard choices....

Paula Steele: Thoroughly accomplished, with a sharp mind, perfect breeding and looks to die for, Paula thrives on challenges and wants to have it all ...
but is this right for her?

Grady O'Connor: Working for Hamilton House was his salvation after Vietnam. The war had messed him up but good and had killed his storybook marriage. He's been given a second chance—only he doesn't know what the hell he's supposed to do with it....

Harlequin Superromance invites you to enjoy Barbara Kaye's dramatic and emotionally resonant miniseries about mature men and women making life-changing decisions. Don't miss:

- CHOICE OF A LIFETIME—a July 1990 release.
  - CHALLENGE OF A LIFETIME
    —a December 1990 release.
- CHANCE OF A LIFETIME—an April 1991 release.

SR-HH-1

Harlequin
Superromance®

A June title
not to be missed....

Superromance author Judith Duncan has created her
most powerfully emotional novel yet, a book about
love too strong to forget and hate too painful to
remember....

Risen from the ashes of her past like a phoenix,
Sydney Foster knew too well the price of wisdom,
especially that gained in the underbelly of the city.
She'd sworn she'd never go back, but in order to
embrace a future with the man she loved, she had to
return to the streets...and settle an old score.

Once in a long while, you read a book that affects you
so strongly, you're never the same again. Harlequin is
proud to present such a book, STREETS OF FIRE by
Judith Duncan (Superromance #407). Her book merits
Harlequin's AWARD OF EXCELLENCE for June 1990,
conferred each month to one specially selected title.

S407-1

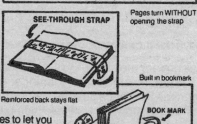

HARLEQUIN
American Romance

THE LOVES OF A CENTURY...

Join American Romance in a nostalgic look back at the Twentieth Century—at the lives and loves of American men and women from the turn-of-the-century to the dawn of the year 2000.

Journey through the decades from the dance halls of the 1900s to the discos of the seventies ... from Glenn Miller to the Beatles ... from Valentino to Newman ... from corset to miniskirt ... from beau to Significant Other.

Relive the moments ... recapture the memories.

Look now for the CENTURY OF AMERICAN ROMANCE series in Harlequin American Romance. In one of the four American Romance titles appearing each month, for the next twelve months, we'll take you back to a decade of the Twentieth Century, where you'll relive the years and rekindle the romance of days gone by.

Don't miss a day of the CENTURY OF AMERICAN ROMANCE.

A CENTURY OF
AMERICAN ROMANCE
1900's

The women...the men...the passions...
the memories....